JUST A CALIFORNIA GIRL

JUST A CALIFORNIA GIRL

Betting on Love #1

NAOMI SPRINGTHORP

Graphic Designer: Irene Johnson johnsoni@mac.com
Editor: Katrina Fair

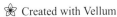 Created with Vellum

For those who survived the Vegas nights we should regret, but don't. Party on. You don't need a chaperone.

PLAYLIST

"Love in an Elevator" by Aerosmith
"Ode to Joy" by Beethoven
"Living on a Prayer" by Bon Jovi
"Dazzey Duks" by Duice
"I Feel Fine" by The Beatles
"Please Please Me" by The Beatles
"And I Love Her" by The Beatles
"We Can Work It Out" by The Beatles
Living In Oz by Rick Springfield
Rock n' Roll Music Volume 1 by The Beatles
"To Be With You" by Mr. Big
"Love of a Lifetime" by Firehouse
"I'll Be There For You" by Bon Jovi
"Heaven" by Warrant
"I Remember You" by Skid Row
"High Enough" by Damn Yankees
"Home Sweet Home" by Motley Crue
"Don't Close our Eyes" by Kix
"Waiting For a Girl Like You" by Foreigner

"I Wanna Be Sedated" by Ramones
"Cum On Feel the Noize" by Quiet Riot
"When I Look Into Your Eyes" by Firehouse
"When You Close Your Eyes" by Night Ranger
"That Was Yesterday" by Foreigner
"Youth Gone Wild" by Skid Row
"All Apologies" by Nirvana
The Best and Beyond by Foreigner
"Play That Funky Music" by Wild Cherry
"Da Ya Think I'm Sexy?" by Rod Stewart
"Tonight's the Night" by Rod Stewart
"Some Guys Have All the Luck" by Rod Stewart
"Always and Forever" by Heat Wave
"Into the Night" by Benny Mardones
"Endless Love" by Diana Ross and Luther Vandross
"Holding On To Yesterday" by Ambrosia
"Jane Says" by Jane's Addiction
"Oh Jackie" (original)
"Get Here" by Oleta Adams
"Crazy" by Aerosmith
"November Rain" by Guns n' Roses
"You Could Be Mine" by Guns n' Roses

CHAPTER ONE

I don't golf! How would I know golfers get out this early? It's not daylight yet. I complained internally as Danny quickly turned around to face the opening elevator doors and backed up toward me, blocking the old guys joining us on the elevator with their golf clubs from catching a visual of my fly undone. Nothing to do about the heavy breathing, and I'm sure I was red with desire. Talk about obvious! Maybe they wouldn't notice. Men, after all, are not the most observant.

Two floors down on level 7 (which I was hoping led to heaven), we got off the elevator. It was a long drawn out walk to my room, he had me pressed up against the wall more than once. I was in a hazy buzzed state that I can only assume Danny was sharing since he had a shiny glint in his eyes and his to die for happy-go-lucky-guy grin spread across his gorgeous face. We would've been acting out Aerosmith's "Love in an Elevator" if it weren't for 5am tee times.

His hands were all over me. Oh, his hands! In my hair, skimming down my back, holding me against him with both of his hands on my ass while his sweet plump lips were kissing me open-mouthed from my forehead, down my neck, and our happy places were grinding together. We got to my room. My best friend had separated from us almost six hours earlier and was sound asleep. Was being key, we woke her up and she kicked Danny out.

"Can't you guys be quiet? Have some respect. I'm sleeping. I have to drive us home and check out is in 5 hours." Jess rattled off in an obnoxious, mad, British accent.

Thankful she actually remembered to use the British accent, I pushed him out the door and went to sleep. Breakfast would be my treat and I had sweet, hot Danny's number in my pocket.

Hmmm... Let's try this again, shall we?

Hi, I'm Jackie and it's the 80s, scratch that—it's the 90s. I miss the 80s, but only because I was young. A minor for all but the last year or so of the 80s and therefore I could always fall back on the fact that I was young and didn't know any better, even though I did. Gotta learn sometime. Sorry. And, the music. Oh, the music! I love 80s rock, pop, punk, metal, new wave— no country. To this day, I'm pining away for my favorite songs I first heard in the 80s. There's always a soundtrack.

You would think I'd learn my lessons. I'd pay attention to what I'm doing. I wouldn't do stupid risky things. I wouldn't put myself in compromising positions. You would think. But, I've always been told to behave and I want to know who this Have person is and why is it I should be like them?

Jess and I should probably not be allowed out alone. Granted she's about a decade older than me, but two confident green-eyed blondes with larger than normal behinds and atti- tudes are going to get noticed. Especially when we pull a stunt like we did this weekend. We truly were doing homework for the choir class we take together. There were simply some unforeseen benefits and I may have taken advantage of them.

Why the maestro chose to give us the eye every time he heard someone whisper during class, I have no idea. It wasn't always us. Yes, we were always in the back row. Yes, we always sat together. Yes, most of the first soprano section was older than us, and silent—there simply as a hobby. We had a performance scheduled only two weeks away and maestro was having fits with the sounds of the words coming out of the huge choir group as a whole. We had recently finished a fantastic season learning and performing Beethoven's *Ode To Joy* in German, and the transition to the English piece we were working on was proving to drive maestro crazy. Funny since he was a tall, thin man with a full head of thick dark hair, we all guessed him to be in his late 30s, and he didn't realize he drove us crazy with his jeans. Yes, jeans. He wore jeans to every practice. High-waisted, snug fitting, straight leg, blue jeans that were faded at the fly and down the left side of his crotch where they outlined his penis and reminded us all he was packing an impressive one.

Maestro scolded us, "You all need to practice a British accent! You don't understand the sound we need for this piece. Watch some British movies. Get together and speak using a British accent. Something! You need to find the sound I'm trying to cultivate from you and make it an everyday skill."

Jess and I discussed our homework assignment while we were driving out of town and heading to Las Vegas for the weekend. Our next practice was Monday night. We decided to do our homework on the way to Vegas and only speak to each other in British accents until we got to the end of the 250 mile drive.

We arrived at the Las Vegas Hilton and pulled in to valet park the dirty old Honda Prelude we were traveling in. I know, off strip. We barely had enough money to go to Vegas for the weekend and we refused to stay at Circus Circus. That's when it happened. The valet walked up to Jess, handed her the ticket with her valet parking info and…

"Thank you my fine sir. I haven't any cash, may I bring a tip a bit later?" Comes piping out of Jess in the most prim, proper, pristine British accent.

The valet replied energetically, "Oh, how long are you ladies visiting and where are you from?"

Remember how I said we shouldn't be allowed out alone?

"We are taking a holiday here for the weekend. We are temporarily working in LA." I said matching Jess' accent.

"We're from Birmingham, England. Working as back up singers in the studios, trying to get more permanent gigs," Jess added to our story.

"Best of luck to you. I'll take meeting you beautiful ladies as my tip," the valet replied.

Jess and I exchanged surprised glances. We grabbed our bags and walked away quickly, giggling to ourselves as we discovered it's going to be hard to stop speaking with a British accent. Four hours to make the habit, days to break it. Why not do extra credit? We continued our completely made up background story, which kept growing in detail, with the accent, for the whole trip—why not have fun in Vegas?

The only plan we had to stick to was what time we needed to leave by to drive home. We had two nights to stay up late, gamble, dance, drink, eat, and roam the strip. It was Friday, Vegas was hopping with people and more celebrities than usual because the Hard Rock Hotel was having its grand opening weekend and had been booked by invitation only, celebs only, and sold out. We knew where we were going, and we would get in.

We got unpacked, figured out what we were wearing for the night and headed to the hotel coffee shop for dinner and keno.

It's amazing how much fun you can have in a coffee shop when the waiter is cute. Or, maybe it was the rum? Whatever. A French dip with a side of fries is even better when served by a slightly dim, tall, thin, dirty blonde hottie. Especially the type with an aptitude for flirting and keeping your glass full. Yes, Jimmy was worth leaving your room key for, or at least a big tip —which if the bulge in his tight fitting Dickies gave any indication, was more than acceptable.

Jess and I both won enough at keno to pay for playing, but not enough to cover dinner—which is what we were hoping for. You should never plan to win when you're gambling. Luck had worked for us before. We had gas money to get home and our room was paid for. The rest of the weekend was all based on luck. We were going for it. We left Jimmy a note with a small tip:

"You deserve more. Your tip should match 'your tip,' which has been a delightful distraction. We'll be back for you, Jimmy. ~Blonde Brits"

We went back to our room and got ready for a night out in Vegas. Completely changing our minds about what we were going to wear and going a bit more extreme. It's Vegas, right?

I dressed in a sheer low cut babydoll top that laced up at the boobs and hung long enough to make you wonder if I was wearing anything underneath it. You couldn't always see if I had black booty shorts on or not. I wore black combat boots, curled my hair and overdid the black eyeliner. I tied a black ribbon around my neck, wearing it as a choker.

Jess always wore pants. She went with skintight black jeans and pulled on a black short-sleeved top with strings to tie at the neck, leaving it untied and essentially creating a V-neck. She flipped her hair around to get some fullness, applied her normal make-up, and stepped into her suede booties.

We did a quick once over to make sure we were Vegas appropriate and took off for the Hard Rock Casino. We were early for Las Vegas standards on purpose. We had a taxi drop us off and walked right into the casino, ready to people watch and check out the celebs.

The Hard Rock Casino floor was basically set up in a circle, if you start walking, it kept going without end. There were cameras set up around the building and different people doing interviews, as well as live music playing in The Joint. The later it got, the fuller it was and the less room there was to move. There was a line of people outside waiting to get in and it wasn't moving. The place was at capacity. A short weaselly comedian was wandering about interviewing other celebrities. The man with the number one song on the pop charts and a couple of brothers that are actors were sitting at a table playing blackjack. Everywhere you turned another famous person popped out of the woodwork, Superman, a slow running life-guard with boobs, and a member of a rowdy heavy metal band. Remember it's the early 90s, these were the A-Listers. We wanted into The Joint, but it was by invitation only and security had stopped us trying to go in twice. We started to flirt with security around the building and worked the situation, but all we could get was an invitation to not get thrown out of the building. We were unquestionably pushing it, using the British accent and our made up back story, saying we knew people, even tried the "but, my Dad's in there" routine. Eventually, we went with it and settled on the celeb watch. We lapped the casino circle numerous times, each time the view changed and different celebrities appeared. Talking to each other and providing personal commentary the whole time. Until, the collision.

I don't know about your opinion, but in the early 90s one of the hottest, most dreamy bachelors on the planet was the hottie doctor from that hospital drama everyone watched. I always thought (and still do) he should get a chance to play James Bond. I get that maybe he doesn't quite fit the stereotype, but have you looked at him? Close enough and add some extra sexy, please!

...And now an interruption to explain one of my infatuations...

I love hot asses. If I have the opportunity to, I will grab, touch, fondle, feel, squeeze, grope, smack, poke, graze a man's hot ass, or sometimes a celeb's ass, to determine if it should be rated as hot, or simply because it's a celeb's ass. What can I say? I have ass issues and I'm not afraid to admit it. I've been to many rock concerts and had the opportunity to rate the goods of the performer. Why would they walk through the crowd if they didn't want to be touched? Okay, grabbed. But, I digress. In fact, we used to play a game at the club where we would make a line of women and snake through the crowd grabbing butts as we made our way from one end of the bar to the other. The fun part was when we didn't tell everybody in the line what we were doing, so we could grab and the girl behind us got blamed. The girl behind me was always irritated because she didn't know the game and couldn't understand why the guys at the club kept turning and glaring at her weird...occasionally finding her later to hit on her under the impression she was interested. Hard, round, perfectly tight globes that look yummy in jeans are my downfall. Lord help me if they are accompanied by a nice package in front with a button fly.

. . .

…And now back to our regularly scheduled program…

Okay, where was I, yes… Jess and I were talking and celeb watching, but apparently I wasn't paying any attention at all to where I was going. Neither was Mr. I'm-super-hot-and-play-a-doctor-on-TV. We were both facing the opposite direction talking to our buddy, while walking opposite directions around the circle of the casino floor and smack! We ran right into each other.

People's Sexiest Man stopped and inspected me, grabbing and holding my arm, "Are you okay?" in his low sexy, oh-my-did-I-just-pass-out, voice.

My brain knocked on itself, h-e-l-l-o is this thing on? Because one of the best ass opportunities ever, and I froze. The immediate response should've been, "Huh? What?" in a sweet breathy voice, including leaning on the hottie to get as much out of the incident as possible. The ass grab needed to happen when the collision occurred, not after he had stopped and spoken to me. Of course, the accent didn't help or have any effect on him. Still, I had a moment with the hot doctor.

We continued to roam the Hard Rock until the crowd became all lookie-loos. It was time for new scenery and the strip was calling our names.

We walked from the Excalibur to Treasure Island, wandering through the casinos and occasionally stopping to watch a lounge act, get a drink, or gamble.

We were propositioned by a guy on the strip because he wanted to have an evening with two blondes. Uh, no.

We played blackjack at the Excalibur and had the best dealer, made $300 in two hours letting him play my hand.

Seems I made more on each hand based on how low my neckline was.

We hung out at Caesars dancing to a lounge act for a while at the barge and a guy told us we were the hottest pair of lesbians he'd ever seen, then came the proposition—he wanted to watch. So, uh no, again. Hello? Not lesbians. I mean Jess and I have made out a couple of times, but it was always for Truth or Dare, or to cause a scene for attention or to get creepy guys to go away. We like men from their ass to their cock and all the muscles in between, their intelligence level simply impacts if they'll get a repeat performance.

We ended the night hanging out watching a live rock band at Treasure Island. They had a tight sound, a unique look, and a lot of energy. We went back to our room when they were done for the night at about 4am. We were out before our heads hit the pillows.

CHAPTER TWO

Saturday we didn't wake up until almost noon and started at Planet Hollywood for lunch. It's in the Forum Shoppes at Caesars Palace, which provides shopping therapy and people watching, besides they have an extensive bar. This is Las Vegas. It's completely acceptable to drink at any hour of the day and we did. The celebrities had overflowed from the Hard Rock and were being spotted everywhere. In fact, we ran into the lifeguard with boobs and the heavy metal guy at three different resorts.

After wandering the Forum Shoppes, eating and drinking lunch, we went back to our room still beat from the night before and played music louder than anybody should in a hotel room. What idiot is going to complain about noise at 4pm? Luckily, nobody. Eventually, we crashed for a couple hours before starting the process over. Getting ready and planning to go back to the Hard Rock again. We got ready early and started at the coffee shop to check-in on Jimmy before heading out for the night.

I wore my favorite, perfect fitting, blue jeans that make my

JUST A CALIFORNIA GIRL

ass look amazing, with my combat boots, and a black snug fitting low scoop neck T-shirt with my black satin push-up bra. I changed up my make-up and went with my dark red lipstick with gold metallic running through it, and gold shadow with my black eyeliner and mascara. Might as well shimmer while I'm in Las Vegas.

Jess followed my lead, going with faded blue jeans and a black V-neck with her booties. Sticking with her norm for everything else and taking my choker.

We walked up to the coffee shop, watching to make sure Jimmy was working before committing to getting a table. Sure enough, he came walking out from the kitchen with a full tray of food, heavy enough to cause his toned and tanned biceps to bulge. We discussed everything else he might have with the ability to bulge, and the potential size of said bulge. Again, Jess and I in Vegas should probably be chaperoned, or possibly not allowed in the State of Nevada. We waved at Jimmy and he immediately sat us in his section, remembering us from last night. Hopefully he doesn't remember the part about us not leaving a tip, or maybe this was our opportunity to make up for it. Being creatures of habit when it comes to food, we ordered the same thing we did the night before. Jimmy was as good, if not better than we remembered, and his service wasn't bad either. Jess picked up the tab and left a special note for Jimmy, with a real tip this time. We hung out, allowing Jimmy to get us refills and flirting for longer than we should have. Vegas is a fluid place and I'm not referring to the free drinks. Sometimes you need to go with the flow. You never know what you might miss.

We got a cab and took off for the Hard Rock, but by the time we got there the line outside had not only started, it was wrapped around the building. It's not happening tonight. We got dropped off at the MGM and started to wander. We started off slow, getting acquainted with the casino and played some black-jack, but the cards weren't friendly. A line started to form for a free lounge act and we went for it. We were in the first bunch to get let in and they gave us a wristband for two free drinks each. Score! The band was already set up and doing a final sound check. The place filled up quickly and they announced the act over the loudspeaker when the singer strutted out on stage looking like a cross between Rod Stewart and Richie Sambora, but older and wearing leopard print. Definition of tacky with big seventies style glasses and a raspy voice. He had a shtick and harassed the crowd obnoxiously. They started to play "Living on a Prayer" by Bon Jovi and got the crowd pumped, but then he goes right back at the crowd. This time complaining about the empty dance floor. After the next song, he stared straight at Jess and I.

"Ladies! Get this place started. I've got a song meant for you, hit the dance floor."

We turned to each other, shrugged our shoulders, and went for it when they started to play "Dazzey Duks" by Duice. There we were, the only two on the dance floor and we didn't care, but the singer did. He called out to the crowd, "What two guys out there want to dance with these beautiful blondes and those luscious asses they've got working?" Seconds later, the oddest pair of guys ambled out onto the dance floor with us. Kind of dancing near us, maybe with us. A tall, good-looking blonde wearing a heavy metal T-shirt who appeared to be about my age and a short chubby guy with a huge dark afro. Black guys were always attracted to us. Which is fine, but not when they're a cock's length shorter than you. We don't do short guys. Jess enjoyed dancing with the afro for a few songs, but got irritated with the attention I was getting from the blonde and started making faces at me communicating her desire to get the hell out of there because, well, she wasn't interested in a short guy who had to be at least 5 years older than her. Before I had to make a move, Metalhead excused himself and I was left wondering, what the fuck? Afro left with him. Jess and I went back to dancing together and enjoying ourselves. By this time, the dance floor had filled up. The band kept playing. A couple of songs later, Metalhead came back and started dancing with both of us, but afro was gone. When the show was over, he told us his buddy had to go to work and Jess was thanking the ceiling. Metalhead, however, had decided to hang out with us.

I'm not going to keep calling him Metalhead. But, I do love metal heads. Heavy metal, old school hard rock, there's not much that compares to it. The way the T-shirt fit his body, stretching at his shoulders and across his chest, well-worn and soft, over snug fitting faded button-fly 501s. Fuck me! About six foot two and solid muscle with light blonde short shaggy hair and warm brown eyes with the ability to melt me easier than a candy bar in the summer. His smile alone could knock your pants off you.

I didn't want to ditch Danny and go play with Jess, he was too good to be true and I needed more time with him. I wanted to find out if he could speak, though I'm not sure I cared. Who am I kidding? I wanted to experience his kiss. I wanted to find out if he tasted as sweet as candy or if his tongue was hot and sinful, hidden behind his happy-go-lucky facade. I wanted his hands on me, and his body against mine. Jess sensed I was into this guy and it didn't happen often. Most couldn't keep my attention, or completely turned me off somehow. She sucked it up like a big girl and the three of us walked across the street to the Excalibur where the drinks were cheaper and the slots were looser.

Danny bought the first round and we started sucking down Midori and Sprites. He ordered and it was the right choice for a night of Vegas drinking. Danny and I stuck to those for the rest of the night and the morning.

A couple hours in at the Excalibur, Jess got tired and said we should go back to our room. I didn't want to and she gave me the eye you get from your mother when you're making a bad decision. Then she wrote LVH and our room number on my hand, making sure I would find it even if I got drunk, and gave me the signal we were cool before she took off.

Danny grabbed my hand and led me off into a secluded spot of the casino where we sat and talked for a few minutes about nothing. He was watching me. He wanted more, to kiss me or something and I wanted him to. He led me to the closed sports book area and leaned against the wall, spreading his feet to bring him down to my height. He pulled me toward him and whispered in my ear, "I don't want to scare you away or push you too far. Something about you, you look like you're my angel and I want to know if you feel like my angel. Let me take you on my Vegas tour." I gazed at him and nodded at his gorgeous frame, with no idea what I was agreeing to. He pressed his lips to my neck, below the ear he'd been whispering in and it tingled down my spine. I reached my arms around his neck and leaned into him. His grin widened, his heart beating against me while his body relaxed at my acceptance. Danny stared directly into my eyes while he kissed me on the lips for the first time. Talk about intense. He watched me, wanting to witness the affect he'd have on me and when I closed my eyes, he took it deeper and licked my lips, parting them so he could stroke my tongue with his. The sweet taste of melon and hot man lingered on my tongue. There was action behind his button-fly, but he didn't acknowledge it. "Definitely my angel,

JUST A CALIFORNIA GIRL

you taste heavenly," he peered down at me with the most devilish hooded dark eyes sneaking through his happy features. He simply wrapped his arms around me and smiled before leading me off to our next destination.

Danny grasped my hand, entangling his fingers with mine as we left the Excalibur and walked out onto the strip. He was talking a mile a minute. "I haven't been living here very long and I've wanted to walk the strip, but nobody who lives here wants to do that. I've been to a few places, but I work at the Stardust and spend most of my time around the North end of town." I listened and went along with his plan. It was obvious he may not be familiar with the casinos we were wandering through, but he knew where to find what he was looking for. We checked out the uniqueness of each casino, shared drinks and found isolated, sometimes dimly lit areas where we sat, talked to each other, touched, kissed, and more as our journey progressed. The whole time, I maintained the British accent with no effort at all.

It became a game to find the dark corner in the casino where we could quietly melt into each other and make out without getting kicked out of the casino or told to get a room. The later it got, the less people there were around and more of the casino areas were closed off. We sat in the back corner of a closed food court talking and simply being close to each other. Touching each other's hands, we sat next to each other with his arm around me, and I leaned my head on his shoulder. We talked about why he moved to Las Vegas and where he was from.

I maintained the British accent and our back-story. I considered telling him the truth, but I was afraid. What if he was interested in me because I was British? What if he simply hates me because the whole thing is a lie? Nothing invested. Too easy to walk away. What does a blonde California Girl who lives less than 300 miles away and always has, possibly have on a musician from England with a sexy accent? At least for the night, I wasn't going to give him up. I was going to keep kissing him, grazing against his body, listening to him talk, making out with him, and getting whisker burn until I had to go home. This is Vegas, and what happens in Vegas stays in Vegas. Right? In all reality, I'll never talk to him again. He'll never find out I'm not British. He'll have a memory of the night he spent on the strip making out with that British chick. I'll have the memory of the night I spent making out with the hot muscled metal head. It's probably better this way, time and reality always fuck everything up.

I learned Danny was not the brightest guy ever, but he made up for it with his honesty, happiness, and good intentions. A real stand-up guy. I needed his refreshing honesty and dependability in my life—his hot body wouldn't be bad either. He worked in the kitchen and janitorial parts of the Stardust, wherever they needed him. He moved to Las Vegas because he wanted to get away from his home on the East Coast. He wanted to experience someplace different, something different, and not be under his mother's thumb. He wanted to be on his own and prove he could make it by himself. He talked to his Mom daily and loved her dearly, even when she tried to get him to move back home. He didn't mind his job, he accepted he had to work his way up and was on track to move into the kitchen. He lived in a motel at the North end of the strip with afro, which he thought was great because he didn't have to clean or wash linens, and afro was on the opposite shift, which meant they rarely crossed paths. He loved heavy metal and the concert opportunities in Las Vegas were something he'd been taking advantage of. Single with no baggage, no significant other, no booty call, and no girlfriend left on the East Coast. He didn't enjoy being alone and told his Mom he would consider moving back home after a year.

The warm masculine claim of his hands on me when he kissed me was life changing. He had passion in everything he did. Never had I experienced this amount of intense passion which wasn't completely sex driven with the guy already getting into my pants. Danny hadn't even tried to touch my bare skin, other than my neck and mouth with his tongue and lips. His muscles bunched when he grazed my breast with his palm or stepped into me feeling my heat on his thigh. The heat between us was palpable. We couldn't keep our hands off each other. We'd be walking through a casino and he'd pull me into a closed sports book area where we'd hide in the individual viewing stations out of sight from any passerby, or up against a wall where you could only see us if you were in the sports book area. His fingers were in my hair while he kissed me and we hid from the rest of the world. Roaming the extremities of the hotels that are mostly empty hallways at this time of day, and taking possession of them to be our own private space to kiss without concern of being in public.

When we got to Harrah's we were going to take the monorail back to my hotel, but it was too late. The monorail had closed for the night. I told him I'd be fine walking back, it was only a mile or so. Danny wouldn't allow it. I wasn't going to be walking in Vegas by myself, he was going to walk with me and I wasn't getting a choice in the matter. The walk was incredible, we were both having a hard time staying awake, still buzzed and our shields were down—we were in our own coupled haze and everything was coming out. He wanted to go out with me again. He wanted my phone number. He said I could stay at his place if I came back for him. He said I was beautiful and I was the reason he moved to Vegas, he just didn't know it until now.

I didn't have a phone number to give him, but I took his and promised to call him in a couple days, adding to the back-story I was going to get a pager soon. In the early 90s most people didn't have cell phones. Many had pagers and some still didn't have either. I hadn't had a need for a pager, but Danny was definitely a need situation. Well, at least he was a need situation in my current buzzed state, with my body buzzing in more ways than one.

When we got to my hotel, we wandered through the Las Vegas Hilton the same way we had the others, and heat built. We wanted each other badly. I don't mean being hungry badly, more stomach growling and I'm going to pass out if I don't eat badly. I mean, we were both having trouble breathing normally. The buttons on his button-fly appeared stressed and they were ready to pop. He not only felt my heat through my jeans, but also how wet I was for him. We managed to get on the elevator and something about it made our condition worse. Heat, no sleep, and an elevator is a sexy situation. Danny put his hands on my hips and backed me to the wall of the elevator, holding me there with his mouth while he unbuttoned my jeans and pulled my zipper down, needy yet tentatively. He was waiting for me to tell him to stop and there's no way that was going to happen. Our hearts were pounding and his pulse was racing, going crazy. He was kissing me hard for the first time. His need getting the best of him and I loved it. He pushed his hand into my jeans and found my wet heat immediately, when the elevator dinged and the door started to open. Danny moved quickly, turned his back to me and backed up against me, blocking the old guys with a 5am tee time from getting an eyeful. I managed to pull my jeans up quickly, but not get them fastened closed. The best part was Danny. His hands were on me, his fingers gently sliding across my heat even for the few seconds he had was fucking fantastic. I have to have him. Right there in the elevator with the golfers and their clubs, he slid his fingers in his mouth and sucked my wetness off of them with a shaky groan. My need grew at the sound of his appreciation, it was all me. I swear his jeans got tighter. We got to the seventh floor and made out like horny teenagers in the hallway, unable to keep our hands off each other. I unlocked the door to my room and Danny followed me in. He said one word and it was over, Jess woke up and yelled at him until he left. I should've been upset at her for cockblocking me, but it was for the best and she was right. We did have to get up and drive home in a few hours. She was driving, but could change her mind and make me do it to get back at me.

I guess you're caught up for the most part. When he was gone, I laid my head down on the pillow and planned to call him in the morning before we left. I'd be getting a pager as soon as humanly possible. If he paged me, I'd recognize the number I was calling back and make sure I used my British accent. I can't believe it, but I think I'll be driving back to Las Vegas soon. The difference a chivalrous walk can make. This may be alcohol induced, but I'll need to visit Vegas soon—for him. I need to find out where this could go. Shit fuck. I like him and want him and he still thinks I'm British. Damn it! Maybe it won't matter. Maybe I'll visit him and find out what happens. Maybe he won't be interested anymore. Maybe it's the Midori and the dancing. Maybe it's his solid body and the way he wears his heavy metal T-shirt. Maybe I'll decide he's a loser when I get to his place because he lives in a motel. Maybe I'm fucked because I like him and I want him and things never work out when they're based on a lie.

CHAPTER THREE

A few hours later I'm rudely awakened by the smack of a pillow to my face, followed by, "Get up! Jimmy is working the coffee shop this morning. We get one more shot at keno and you're buying breakfast." Jess is glaring at me with a familiar expression that tells me she's in charge and I know better than to object to her demand. Unfortunately, I fall back to sleep.

"Jackie, get up! You're not making me miss breakfast with Jimmy." She's insistent.

"Okay, I'm getting up. What's with breakfast with Jimmy?" I wait for a response. She's not acting mad or even irritated with me. In fact, could it be... "Jess, did you have sex with Jimmy?"

"Damn it. You aren't supposed to know that."

"Why not?" I query.

"I can't make it your fault when I'm tired because you woke me up bringing the hot guy back to our room if I was busy with Jimmy until about an hour before you got back to the room. And, what were you bringing him here for? Were you going to do it with him while I was in the room?"

JUST A CALIFORNIA GIRL

We know each other too well. "I'm going with I was drunk and he's hot. Excuse? Yes, but I'm playing that card anyway."

Jess shot me a disapproving glance.

"In case you missed the recap, you had sex and I didn't." I point out to her plainly. "At least we don't need to leave him a tip," I say laughing.

She lets out an exasperated sigh and gestures for me to hurry up and get ready.

"So, I'm guessing he was fun?" Trying to find out about her experience with Jimmy. "I mean he was a gorgeous sight, what was he packing?"

Jess didn't appreciate my line of questioning and kept motioning for me to hurry up.

Suddenly, memories of last night and Danny steal my focus.

"Why did your facial expression change?" She stares at me oddly.

"What do you mean?" having no clue what she's talking about.

"What are you thinking about and did it just change?" She's too observant. Shit. We really do know each other too well.

"Umm, nothing."

"Don't make me go over there. I have a pillow and I'm not afraid to use it," harmlessly threatening me.

"Danny. I like him, he told me all about himself, and he thinks I'm British. I want him and this can't go well."

"He's Vegas fun. Forget about him. We're going home and you won't see him again anyway," Jess spouts off.

"What about Jimmy? Vegas fun and never seeing him again?" I ask bitchily.

"Jimmy is buying us breakfast, if you would hurry up and get moving," Jess still avoids the question.

I roll out of bed, pull on some jeans and a T-shirt, and slip on my flip-flops. "I'm ready."

"Seriously?" She looks me up and down.

"I'm not trying to impress anybody, you already slept with Jimmy."

Jess smacks me and drags me out to the coffee shop where Jimmy has a table waiting for us. I concentrate on keno and let them play whatever game they're playing with each other. I'm happy I'm not buying breakfast. I break away to find the ladies room, but it's simply an excuse and I'm in search of a pay phone. I want to know if Danny gave me his real number.

"Hello?" a much higher pitched voice than Danny's comes over the phone. A woman?

"Hi, uh, is Danny there?"

"No, he's at work."

"Oh, wow. Okay, will you please let him know I called? This is Jackie." On second thought, "Actually, never mind I'll call him back."

"He's off tomorrow. He'll be happy you called," and he hangs up.

He was up with me all night, even walked me to my room, and is already at work. Shit! He even had to walk home. Poor Danny. I don't know how he can do it.

He did give me his real phone number. I want to see Danny again, I need a chance to be with him. Tomorrow I'm getting a pager. I can already hear Jess reading me the riot act.

I get back to breakfast to find Jimmy sitting at the table with Jess, his arm around her shoulder and his lips pressed to her neck, buried in her hair. When I approach she raises her eyebrows a couple times at me, conveying a "woo woo, Jimmy is hot" to me in our silent language. Now, I would think it's strange to have a waiter sit down at my booth at his work and start kissing me at any time of day, let alone on a Sunday morning, but this is Las Vegas and anything goes. I signal her trying to find out if I should turn around and walk away, but my breakfast is sitting on the table waiting for me and I opt for the food, picking up my plate and taking it with me to the breakfast counter. Jess will find me when she's ready.

Hope suddenly slaps me across the face. Maybe we can stay another night. Jess can play with Jimmy and I can play with Danny. We were strapped to make the trip in the first place, but we won money on the trip. Sunday night has got to be cheaper, right? Crap. We both have to work tomorrow and reality once again is a bitch, always deflating my mood and taking away my fun.

I finish breakfast and my third cup of coffee. Jess finds me at the counter and pulls me from the coffee shop quickly. "We have to get out of here. He wants me to hang out for his break to uh, yeah. Let's get out of here."

I glance at Jess when we step into the elevator and she responds before I ask my question, "We can't. We have work tomorrow. Yes, he's adorable and sets me on fire. I'm not taking any chance on getting attached to him. He's a waiter."

This would be an appropriate time to tell you about Jess. She's been burnt by guys more than any other female I've ever met. They're married, or they come out of the closet or they give a fake name and fake number, or they want to get into a fist fight with you, or they're intimidated by you when they get beyond the sex, or they marry you and knock up another woman, or they accidentally knock you up and disappear. Yep, Jess has experienced them all and now, she keeps them all at arms length. She has her own kind of use them and abuse them, catch and release program. Jimmy is the closest to a second date

I've seen in years, I was surprised she agreed to breakfast. Though, free breakfast is hard to pass up.

We get our things packed up, call the valet for the car, and check out. As soon as we get settled in the car and hit the freeway toward Los Angeles, Jess starts in, "Were you seriously considering staying another night for a guy? It doesn't make any sense, you already know it'll go bad. It's all based on a lie."

"He gave me his real number and he had to go to work this morning after walking me to our room, and he had to walk home. He's working on pretty much no sleep because he was with me and chivalrous."

"And, he wanted to get laid," Jess says jaded.

"So did I. Cockblocker," I say laughing.

"I'm sure you can get laid easily at home," Jess makes weird eyes at me insinuating I should call one of my many on call guys.

"I want Danny."

"Do what you want, but it's going to turn out bad," She says matter-of-factly. "You're not one to get hooked on a guy. I don't want you to end up hurt."

Jess is right, but it's not going to stop me. So, I'm not British. It's more of a fib than a lie. I mean it doesn't hurt anyone. I'll need to come clean when I see him next time. Maybe after we have sex. Can I pull off British while having sex? None of it matters. I'm going to be with Danny again and I'm going to have him alone with me naked.

CHAPTER FOUR

I t was a long ride home. Our later than planned start planted us right smack dab in the middle of traffic. I napped part way home and drove halfway, giving Jess a chance to sleep. She drops me off and I have a male friend sitting on my doorstep waiting for me. She shakes her head, "My point has been made."

"I'm getting a pager tomorrow and calling Danny."

Jess and I say our goodbyes and she drives off, shaking her head at the choice I've made. I check out the guy waiting at my door and wonder how my life got here. Okay, fine. I have a boyfriend, Rob, but only because he doesn't take me seriously when I break up with him. I've dumped him at least six times and he laughs at me. I don't live with him or anything, but when he comes over, well, what girl in her right mind turns away a guy who knows how to use his tongue and always wants to worship her?

Funny thing, the guy on my doorstep isn't Rob who doesn't believe I'm really dumping him. It's moody, emotional, Bryan, and he's sitting there playing his acoustic guitar. Rob's mad at

me because I went to Vegas without him and he doesn't want
me to hang out with Jess, he's probably ignoring me on purpose
for a few days. I couldn't care less, it's more of a reward. Bryan,
on the other hand, is a lot of fun and I'm referring to more than
in the bedroom or on the kitchen counter or bent over the
balcony railing. He's cool to hang out with and play music. His
guitar skills are excellent and when he brings his acoustic with
him, he's hoping I'll sing with him while he plays. This also
means he's emotional about something. He may have fucked his
current conquest or broke-up with a girl he'd been dating for the
last week, or any number of male issues. Musicians are often
emotional, especially if they write their own music and Bryan is
a prolific songwriter. I invite Bryan in and spend the evening
playing music and singing with him. He's totally digging my
British accent and thinks it's funny that I'm having a hard time
stopping. He's even choosing songs for me to sing with him
from the British Invasion, which is perfect because I love the
Beatles and it's his way of teasing me about the accent, possibly
making me use it more. It's a great evening. Fun and relaxing,
until he leans in to kiss me and take the evening into a different
direction. Usually I'm happy to humor Bryan with whatever he
wants, because he's a hot musician and I've always believed we
would eventually end up together, but not tonight. Tonight,
when Bryan touches me it doesn't leave my skin heated the way
Danny's hands did, when Bryan kisses me it doesn't send chills
down my spine the way Danny's lips did, and I can't get into it.
I'm not interested. I send Bryan on his way and tell him I'm
tired, maybe I'm getting sick. Truth is I must be sick because
I'm allowing myself to get this hooked on a guy in Vegas and he
doesn't even know who I am. I'm fucking screwed!

The next day after work, I go to a couple places and
compare pagers. I find a place willing to give me a cheap deal

on the pager and I go for it. I test the pager to make sure it works and go out in search of a somewhat secluded pay phone.

I should explain something about pay phones here. I realize no place has pay phones and if they do they're emergency call boxes on the side of the road or used for drug deals or maybe hiding in the back of a hotel. Maybe now, but then there were pay phones everywhere. I mean every restaurant, every grocery store, almost every retail establishment had a pay phone outside the door and sometimes in the back next to the restrooms.

I go to my favorite Mexican take-out place and order, while I'm waiting I use the pay phone in the back to call Danny. I dial his number and hope he answers.

"Hello?" It sounds like it might be Danny.

"Hi, is Danny there?" I ask with a pristine British accent.

"Hey Jackie! This is Danny. I didn't know if you'd call. I hoped you would." The inherent happy-go-lucky in his voice.

"I'm calling to give you my pager number and I was thinking about taking you up on your offer to visit and stay with you," wondering how he'll respond.

"I'm off Friday and don't have to be to work until 2pm on Saturday, hold on…" I listen while he puts the phone down and talks to his roommate, "My roommate works Friday night, we'd have the place to ourselves from about 11pm until 9am."

"Are you sure you want me there? You just met me. I probably couldn't get there until late Friday evening, a bit after supper." Questioning him and my own judgment for considering going to his place when I only spent one night drinking and making out with him. I don't know him.

"Yes. I've been thinking about you. We can order pizza when you get here or go out or stay in, whatever you want." He gives me his address and a plan is made. "I can't wait for Friday." All I can do is smile.

Monday I go to bed happy, anticipating time with Danny on Friday. I don't tell Jess I got a pager and I'm going back to Vegas, though I'm not sure she wouldn't want to join me to get some Jimmy. I do tell Dot, since she's been harassing me to get a pager for months. Dot swears I'll end up chopped into chunks and dumped into the aqueduct if I continue dating guys I meet online, and I've been doing a lot of online dating—it's fun, the guys have above average jobs, and they buy me dinner. She's taken on the role of my keeper and lives only a few blocks away from me. Dot is married, conservative, and if you ask me I'd say she's living vicariously through my adventures. What can I say? I have fun. I can attest, it's absolutely true, blondes do have more fun.

Tuesday is the slowest workday ever. There's something to be said for busy days with consistent customers, at least they go quickly and they allow me to make extra money. Something in my pocket vibrates and it's a new sensation, not something I've experienced before. What the hell? Oh, my pager! I'm at work, but it's slow. I take a peek at the number and sure enough it starts with 702—Las Vegas. It's almost 2:30pm, I quickly take my afternoon break and disappear into the back office to find a phone with some privacy. I don't want to answer questions about why I'm using a British accent.

I dial the number showing most recent on my pager, "Hello?"

"Hi, uh, somebody paged me?" I say in a British accent.

"Hi, Jackie. It's Danny. I hope you don't mind me paging you," he says with his voice showing something more than his happy-go-lucky personality.

"Actually, you made my day," I reply with a giggle.

The sound of his smile is clear, "I wanted to hear your voice."

Oh, fuck. Not just my voice. I need to find out more, "My voice? Is it the only part of me you're interested in?"

"No. I'm interested in the whole package, the voice is all I can have today," Roughness takes over in his voice. I have hope.

The rest of the day was a blur. My mind was stuck on the Danny Daydreaming Channel and his desire overtaking his happy-go-lucky tone on the phone. I remember the heat of him brushing against my skin. I can smell his fresh clean man scent. I can taste him and the melon liqueur on my lips. I go straight home after work, unable to focus on anything other than Danny. My level of need is at an all-time high. I want to call him, but I don't want to be needy and I don't want to be one of those annoying clingy girls, I manage to talk myself out of it. I focus on getting to the weekend and start the packing process. Interesting, what do I want to wear? Should I take lingerie? No, too contrived, he doesn't need to think I planned it. I'll wear my black sexy lace bikini panties and matching bra, since he seems like a man who would appreciate unwrapping a package. I'll pack an outfit for going out on the strip, extra jeans, a couple T-shirts, a hoodie, sweatpants, flip-flops, and I always have my sneakers in my truck, in case of emergency. I'll go with my tight jeans, leather boots and my sleeveless black deep V-neck top. This will give me options for whatever we do, and something appropriate for when his roommate is home. I go to bed before I do something stupid and lose my ability to control myself.

Wednesday is slower than Tuesday and it's killing me. I decide to reward myself by calling the number from yesterday at the same time. 2:30pm can't get here soon enough. My co-worker goes home sick, which helps the time pass quicker. All of a sudden it's 2:35 and I can't believe I missed my mark. I go on break quickly and call the number, hoping he answers and he doesn't decide I'm crazy.

"Hello?" It's him.

"Hi, Danny," I say sweetly in accent.

"Hey Jackie," Danny smiles.

"I hope it's okay I called. I wanted to hear your voice," I repeated his line from yesterday back at him.

"You call me whenever you want. This number is the break room at my work," He says with satisfaction in his voice.

I laugh happily at the affect I have on him by doing something trivial and calling him unsolicited. I don't want to play any more games with him on top of what I've already done. "I was thinking about you yesterday after we talked."

"Yeah? What were you thinking?" His raspy tone has already taken over and I can envision the dirty glint in his eye.

"I'm not sure I should say those things over the phone." I say softly. "It might be rated R or X and we're on a work phone."

"Please do," he says with obvious interest.

"I was remembering how your warm hands make my skin hot and my nerves tingle. I fell asleep last night with the taste of you and Midori on my tongue," I confess sexily.

There's a groan on the other end of the phone. I may have hit a nerve. "Tell me more." He wants to hear it all.

"I'm at work and so are you. It's probably not a smart idea," trying to use my brain.

"I wish it was Friday," Danny whispers, "I want you. I want to kiss you again and taste your sweet lips. I want to put my arms around you and hold you against me." His heat is coming through the phone.

"I can't wait to be with you. I'll try to get off work early on Friday. Are you busy later?"

"I'll be waiting for you whenever you get here. I'm off work at 8pm tonight," he says.

"It's probably best if we don't continue this line of conversation, until we're in the same room with each other," I suggest.

He laughs, "I don't want you to think I'm something better than I am, but I'd be happy to listen to what you want."

"Danny, are you a dirty boy?" I ask teasingly.

"Only if you want me to be, and I'm pretty sure you do," he says hitting the nail on the head.

"I'm not sure what kind of a girl you think I am," making him wonder.

"You're the girl I want," he says as if there's no question and as long as I'm there everything will be right. His steady, sincere voice churns up butterflies in my stomach.

It's a good thing he's on a break and had to disconnect. He makes me a hot and bothered pile of mush, completely useless unless you're Danny and want sex.

I immediately get permission to leave work early on Friday and I'll be kissing Danny in about 48 hours.

8:30pm and my pager is vibrating again. I check the number and it's Danny. I contemplate ignoring him, maybe I shouldn't always be available. Why torture myself? I call him.

"Hello?" I'm not sure about the voice who answers.

"Hi, um, somebody paged me?"

"It wasn't me, hold on…"

"Jackie?" His familiar happy voice comes through clearly.

"Hey Danny, I got your page," sounding upbeat.

"I was thinking we might continue our conversation from earlier, but my roommate walked in," he was hoping for phone sex.

"Oh? Well, I guess I could tell you some things I've been

dreaming. Though I guess it might not be nice of me. I don't want to be a tease."

"Jackie, I want you so bad. I don't think anything is going to make it worse. Tony is getting ready to get in the shower, why don't you start talking and we can see what happens from there?"

"First, I may be there earlier on Friday, maybe 5pm depending on the bloody traffic. Now, let me, umm…" I pause to decide how far I want to take this.

"You know I can't stop thinking about the elevator and the way you broke into my jeans to touch me. It's a memory I've been replaying in my head. Your hand on my bare privates and your fingers fondling my pussy for that brief moment was hot, I'm hoping you'll touch me again. Do you think you might want to touch me again?" Asking him a question he can answer without giving away the conversation on purpose.

"Yes. More than you know," he says and I can detect the heat.

"I want to kiss you for hours. I want to sit on your lap facing you, kissing you, and sucking your tongue into my mouth. I want your cock to rub against me through your jeans while I kiss you, I want you to get hard for me. I want you to need me so much you can't keep your hands off of me, you want to feel my breasts and put your hand down my pants uncontrollably. Danny?" I need some feedback, I need to know what's going on there. "Danny? Did I get disconnected?" I'm not getting a response.

"I'm here," he says. "Tony went in the bathroom to shower. I couldn't talk with him here." His breathing is heavy. "Do you really want me or are you playing with me on the phone?"

"I told you, I'm not a tease."

"I may need to trade my Saturday shift and spend the whole weekend with you."

"Danny, tell me how your cock would feel," I want to hear his words.

"Right now, it's hard as a rock. I could use it as a fucking hammer."

"Like a jackhammer? You could break concrete?"

"Yes, that's better than what I was thinking. I'd love to show you what I can do with my jackhammer."

"Oh? What would you do?" I ask playing dumb.

There's a low groan, "I'd kiss you and make out with you. I'd want you sitting in my lap facing me. I'd work your jeans with my fingers and put my hand in your pants, my other hand holding your mouth to mine. I'd release my hammer from my jeans and slide you slowly down on top of me, filling you with my cock. I'd hold your hips, pushing you down on me while I push up into you hitting your sweet spot. And yes, I'm long enough to reach it and so thick that it'll take time to get there as you stretch around me.

Oh, fuck me. "Danny, wrap your hand around your cock and stroke it for me slowly, firmly. I'm wet for you right now. You make me so hot. Stroke it, Danny. Feel your tight grip and imagine how I'll be hot, wet, and tighter around you. I'll be pressing my lips to yours and sliding my tongue into your mouth. I'll be dragging my fingers across your back, biting at your ear. I'll be moving on you, sliding down onto your hard cock until there's no more cock to slide in, then pulling off of you slowly, over and over. Stroking your huge cock with my heat." I listen for Danny.

"You're a bad girl." He's out of breath and can hardly speak.

"Only because you want me to be," I quickly reply. "Don't you want it?"

"You're amazing and you're not even here, oh fuck…" I hear the phone drop.

A few seconds later, "Baby, you there?" Danny asks.

"Of course, are you?"

"Not so much. Fuck. Are you getting off?" Danny asks.

"No. I'm waiting for you. I'm hot and I want you. I'm going to be so tightly wound, all you'll have to do is look at me."

"I'm going to make you go off so many times, you won't be able to stand," in his I-mean-it tone and it drives me crazy.

Thursday went quickly. After work, I finished laundry and got my things packed for the weekend. I called Dot and reviewed my plans with her. I gave her Danny's address and she didn't approve of me going to a guy's place I met in Las Vegas only last weekend. She argued that I don't know him from Adam. She also had issues with the fact he lives in a motel and the address I gave her is not in the best location. I told her I'm not going to be alone there, Danny will be there and he'll protect me. Dot continued to be leery, I went on and described Danny: tall, solid, muscled, blonde, brown-eyed, hottie… and suddenly it was okay. I'm supposed to page her my special code when I get there, to confirm I get there in one piece. She has a code for everything, it's like calling an audible at the line of scrimmage. It's always about pieces with her, I need to be in one piece instead of chopped into pieces and she wants all the details about his "piece".

CHAPTER FIVE

I wake up nervous on Friday, or maybe I'm anxious. I go to work and have a note on my desk saying I can leave when my co-worker gets back from lunch. Yay! I'll be out of here before 1pm. I start talking to the old lady, I mean my co-worker, about recipes and food, trying to get her to go to lunch earlier than normal by subliminally making her hungry.

I get my work done quickly and start in on my follow-up calls, trying to close some sales and make some extra cash. I clean my desk up, and I'm ready to go as soon as the old lady gets back from lunch. I shouldn't have had two cups of coffee. I'm running at two hundred miles per minute. She goes on her lunch break and I cover her desk. Which basically means I sit there twiddling my thumbs and making drawings, while I wait for the phone to ring or somebody to walk through the door. I review my scribbles and I have a list on the right side of every-thing I've packed, on the bottom left I have the math figuring out what time I'll get there based on the number of miles and my approximate ETD (Estimated Time of Departure), and all over the rest of the page I've written Danny in about fifty different ways.

I can't believe I'm going to drive to Las Vegas for a man. I always make guys come to me, well unless it's a first date. I try to make sure they're not crazy before I tell them where I live. Honestly, I usually meet guys at a public location and never take them to my apartment. But this, driving over 250 miles for a dude? This is out of character. Then again, Danny isn't any guy off the street. We spent over eight hours together, that counts as a first date, right? And, he was so chivalrous. He gave up his sleep for me and walked miles farther for me. Not to mention—he's one of the hottest guys ever and kisses like a dream. No, I'm not out of character, my character has simply taken on a British accent and enough guilt to make the drive without a second thought.

My co-worker is standing over me and I wonder how long she's been there. She motions for me to get out and I don't need to be told twice. I'm off for the weekend. I make a quick stop in the private back office to call Danny.

"Hello?" a female voice answers the phone.

"Hi, is Danny there?" it must be Tony's girl.

"Housekeeping, nobody here right now," she says rudely in broken English.

"Can you leave a message for Danny?" I ask politely.

"I try," she says and hangs up.

That didn't go well. I fill up my gas tank, pick up my duffle bag, and hit a drive thru for lunch on the road. Driving to Vegas from LA is madness, especially on Fridays. Everybody and their brother, mother, aunts, uncles, and cousins are on the 15 Freeway to Las Vegas. The later it gets, the more cars are on the road. I'm hoping I've left early enough to miss most of the traf-fic. I pop my Rick Springfield *Living in Oz* CD in and turn the volume up, driving with the windows down and singing at the top of my lungs the whole way there.

I get to Baker and the World's Tallest Thermometer in record time. The only issue being the two mile stretch of highway where my truck was pelted with insects and I had to roll up the windows to keep them on the outside, whatever they were. Seems most of them are smashed somewhere on my truck. There's about an hour more to drive before I hit Nevada if the traffic stays good, which is only forty minutes the way I drive. I pull off the freeway to wash my windows and find a payphone. I dial Danny's number…

"Hello?" Tony answers.

"Hi, is Danny there?"

"No, is this Jackie?" he asks.

"Yes," I say wondering where the hell he is.

"One of our co-workers needed someone to trade shifts with him, so Danny did it because it gives him Saturday and Sunday off. He should be home about 5pm. I'm supposed to find out what time you're getting here if I talk to you," Tony fills me in.

"Oh, I'm in Baker now and I'll probably get there before he's off work. Please have him page me when he gets home." I can always find something to do in Vegas, but I'm not going to wait at his place with Tony.

"You're going to be driving past the Stardust on your way here. Danny's anxious to see you. He gets off work at 4:30pm and always exits through the side door to walk home. I'm guessing you might be anxious to see him, too."

"Thank you, Tony. I'll see what time I get there."

I switch the CD out to The Beatles *Rock n' Roll Music Volume 1* and continue my drive. There's something therapeutic about driving with the windows down, the warmth of the sun on my skin, the music blaring, my hair blowing in the wind, and singing at the top of my lungs. It makes me feel free. It makes me forget everything negative. It makes me relax. Add the old school beats and grooves, and my cheeks hurt from smiling.

I pull off the freeway at the state line exit for some last minute preparations. I use the bathroom at the gas station to change my clothes and freshen up before I get to Danny, making sure I'm perfect when I meet him. I brush out my windblown hair, change my top, and pull on my boots. I buy a soda, because more caffeine is what I need right now. I get hit on twice when I'm leaving the gas station mini mart. I double check myself in the mirror to make sure I don't have my shirt on backwards or something and realize I might look that good. My happy attitude adds to it.

My anticipation of being with Danny has me buzzing. I hope I haven't built him up in my mind into something he isn't. I remember how he felt in person. His hands on me were amazing and affected me more than any others from my past. The softness of his lips and the playfulness of his tongue. The warmth of his happy-go-lucky gaze on me. How his eyes and expression change with his heart and need toward desire. I want to be there and see his face when his tone turns to the gravelly groan I heard over the phone. I want to read his eyes when he uses his I-mean-it tone.

I need to tell him I'm not from England, I'm just a California Girl. I'm a musician, but not a studio singer. I do more than sing with choir groups. I give music lessons, teaching mostly music reading and piano to kids. I've been pulled up on stage at the local clubs to sing back-up vocals for the cover bands and I've met most of the guys who play locally. I've been in a couple of bands, but none of them have been serious enough to be worth my time and effort. I would love to get into studio work. But, for now, most of my music industry time is spent in the warehouse doing phone sales to record stores. Yes, I sit in an office and call music stores all over the country selling them stock from all different genres—everything from pop and rock to country and classical, formats from vinyl and 8-track to cassette singles and CDs. So, I'm not a complete lie. I've shown Danny my real personality, my real heart. He's kissed my lips and that's all me. I'm going to push away the horrible feeling that he'll hate me and ignore it until it's the right time. I want a chance to be with him before I tell him. It could be a deal breaker.

I put it all out of my mind while I drive the highway from state line to the Las Vegas Strip. I get back to singing and my happy mood, only with the windows up to keep from getting windblown again. I check the time and I can make it to the Stardust before Danny gets off work. I'm not sure it's the best idea, but Tony suggested it and I'm going with it.

CHAPTER SIX

I pull into the Stardust parking lot and drive around in search of the side door. Sure enough, there's a side door labeled employees. I park about thirty feet from the door with nothing blocking the view, get out and lean on my truck with my feet crossed waiting for my hottie to come walking out. I feel sexy in my tight fitting, faded black jeans, and black V-neck—showing all my curves. I'm sure it shows in my stance and my attitude. Why shouldn't it? He wants me. I double-check the time and it's 4:25pm, only a few more minutes and I can't wait to be near him.

4:31pm and people start trickling out the door, some obviously happier than others to get away from work. People of all ages, ranging from their early 20s to elderly octogenarians. It's odd co-workers could have such an extremely different attitude when leaving the same place of employment, some happy and ready to go party while others look like death warmed over. A few minutes have gone by and a couple of the guys are hanging outside the door.

About 4:40pm one of the somewhat creepy guys comes

walking over to me rather aggressively and starts talking about half way to me, "Hey, baby. Are you waiting for me? We should go party." His greasy voice confirms he's a total creeper.

Before I can jump in my truck, lock the door, and drive away, a familiar voice both puts me at ease and causes my tummy to flutter at the same time. "Forget it, she's mine," Danny yells out. His tone decisive, protective, and claiming. "Hey, baby! I didn't expect you this early." Grinning from ear to ear, his smile alone does me in.

Creepy leers at Danny, "She's yours? Seriously, new guy? I want to hear it from her."

What a fucking jackass! Challenging Danny isn't a smart idea, but I guess he's more a lover than a fighter.

Danny focuses on me with a more serious expression on his face and his voice goes raspy, "Are you mine, baby?" He's actually asking me the question.

In my pristine British accent, "Of course, Danny. I wouldn't drive over 250 miles for you if I wasn't." I beam an uncontrollable smile at him and the butterflies continue to flutter with anticipation. "Now, get over here and claim me."

Danny steps in front of the creepy guy, plasters his body up against mine and kisses me silly. Making his point clear to the creep and anybody else who was getting any ideas, I'm his. I'm his, wow. I'm stunned by the instant connection and heat. I don't even kiss him back, it's all him taking me and I'm not complaining. I love it! Danny pulls on my door handle and says, "Let's get out of here." We drive off leaving the creepy guy in awe.

"I guess picking you up at work wasn't the best idea," I say cautiously.

"Not the safest thing to do, considering some of the guys I

work with. But, I can't blame them. You're beautiful." My cheeks warm and his eyes shine as he gazes at me.

"Tony suggested I pick you up on my way by, since I'm early."

"I liked seeing you there waiting for me. If you do it again let me know and I'll go out the front way. Let's go to my place. I want to wash work off and take you out." He reaches his arm around me while he directs me to his place.

We pull into the parking lot of an old two-story no-tell motel and park in front of his room. Danny leads me in to a room with two king size beds, a bathroom, a dresser, a TV, and a small table with three chairs off in the corner on the far end of the room. Not much extra space, the room is basically beds and walkways. It's clean and there are neat stacks of clothes, magazines, and such around the room. There are beams on the ceiling, adding some character to the space. Danny's bed is the one next to the door, he's got a boom box with heavy metal stickers on it sitting on the window ledge. Tony's sitting on his bed watching TV, it's obvious he's been living here longer than Danny. Danny excuses himself to shower and wash off work. Tony makes small talk and tells me about the building, how they're converting it to apartments starting with their half of the building being rented out by the week. Only in Las Vegas. The room isn't great, but it's clean and cheap. What do I care? I'm not paying to stay there. I sit on Danny's bed watching whatever Tony has on the TV and waiting for Danny to emerge from the bathroom.

Danny comes strolling out of the bathroom with a towel around his waist. Wet hair hanging in his eyes, all of his muscles there for me to drool over, and the sexiest tattoo I've ever seen. A tattoo of a tiger stretching up his left side, almost climbing his chest up to his left shoulder. I'm not a tattoo girl, but it's so fucking sexy. It makes me want to lick it and him from head to toe. I do my best to maintain control, but Danny catches the heat in my eyes, he wasn't thinking coming out of the bathroom mostly naked. Or, maybe he was. He pulls on his Levi's going commando and grabs a Quiet Riot T-shirt from a stack on the dresser. He hangs the towel over his head and rubs his hair dry before pulling the shirt over his head. I sit there and watch his muscles dance with his movements and his ass is amazing in his snug fitting jeans, I know he hasn't buttoned up yet even though he's facing the other direction.

Tony takes the scene in and starts, "Are you guys going out or staying in?"

"I was thinking I'd take her to the pizza place," Danny says.

"Why don't you two talk about it while I get ready in the bathroom," Tony winks at Danny telling him to pay attention, there's a woman sitting on your bed waiting for you.

Tony disappears into the bathroom and Danny turns to me. I smile at him and he sits next to me, putting his hand on the back of my neck and pulling me to him slowly. He gazes into my eyes, "I didn't want our first kiss to be like it was in the parking lot. That was all show, for my co-workers." He presses his soft lips to mine gently, lightly sucking on my lower lip, then my upper lip. He traces my lips with his tongue and I open for him. His once playful tongue gives me much more and asks for much more than it had before. Without hesitation I respond to his kiss, matching his desire and intensity. He pulls me against him, not allowing enough space for even air to penetrate us, and leans us down to the bed with him over me. Our kiss is heated, the weight of his body on mine is somehow sensual and driving my need. His heart is racing while his mouth devours mine. His hands simply hold me where he wants me, as if I'm a dish of his favorite food and he's starving. I run my fingers through his damp hair and down his back, exploring his solid muscles. His skin is smooth and he smells like hot fresh man. I reach his ass and squeeze a cheek with each hand, while I give his tongue a suck. His breath turns ragged and he gets harder against my leg. He stops and pulls away, searching my eyes for something, permission maybe or wondering if we're in the same place. Suddenly the bathroom door opens and Tony wanders out. Danny rolls off of me quickly to his side, pretending we were lying there talking. There's no way Tony buys it, I'm sure we're both red and you can't hide the heavy breathing.

"I'm going to grab my wallet and get out of here. Just pretend I didn't interrupt and enjoy your evening. Remember food and water are important. Don't forget to use a condom." The motel room door shut and locked behind Tony as he left for the evening.

We both laugh at Tony and Danny asks me, "Are you hungry? I want to take you out to eat and pick up some drinks for later."

"I'm hungry, but not for food." My eyes are on him with serious intent. "Take your shirt off. I want to get a closer look at your tattoo, Tiger."

"Are you sure you want me to take my shirt off? I might not want to put it back on," flames shine in Danny's eyes. "Once you let the Tiger out, he doesn't want to be caged."

"I know how to order delivery, so unless there's a condom shortage take off your shirt or I'll do it for you," sounding like a nasty schoolmarm with the accent.

Danny reaches for a bag on the side of his bed and pulls out a brand new box of large sized condoms. "I don't want to push you. You didn't drive to Las Vegas for me to play with your body. I like you and I think it's obvious that I want you, but sex would be a bonus," he says as he adjusts his cock in his jeans.

"I understand you're off work for the whole weekend, is that correct?" I try to get the details straight.

"Yes, I have to work at midnight Sunday night," Danny answers.

"And, I can stay here with you until you go to work late Sunday without being a problem or intruding on other plans? I'm sure I'm not the only girl in your life."

"Tony will be around some, but he works all weekend and we can go out. If you're okay with that, then please stay with me," knowing everybody isn't fond of his roommate. "I haven't been with a woman since I got to Vegas three months ago and I'm not inviting any others back to my place."

"Then, we should use our time wisely and I'm giving you a bonus." I smile at him, making my intentions obvious. "Time for everything else later." I reach for his shirt and pull it off over his head. I want to inspect his tiger tattoo in great detail, with my tongue.

Danny stares at me unsure and not moving. Finally he speaks, "All I've wanted to do all week is kiss you and slide into you, baby."

"I'm sorry if you find me selfish. I'm starting with this tiger. We'll get to everything else. I want you, Danny." I'm completely focused on the tattoo, it's been driving me crazy. Kneeling on the bed, face to face I reach my lips up slightly to meet his and kiss him tenderly. I drag a line of kisses from his mouth, down his neck to his left shoulder at the top of the tiger. His body trembles. He doesn't know what to do with his hands. My hands are holding his body, one on each of his sides at chest level as I kiss his collarbone. This hot, confident man, unsure in my hands is driving my desire. I move my hands along his body, caressing up and down his sides as I trace the inked lines of the tiger with my tongue, stopping to kiss the special spots along the way. Savoring every line as I lick his body. Danny is silently enjoying the process, the bulge behind his button fly causing the fit to get noticeably tighter. I move my hands to his fly and undo the top button nimbly while my tongue continues it's travels. I trace the tiger's tail as it curls up toward his nipple, it's an arrow directing me where to go next. I run my flattened tongue over his nipple and kiss it sweetly with my lips while I undo the second button on his fly drawing a low groan from Danny. He moves his hips and I undo the third button. I slide my hand into his jeans, grasping his hard length and releasing him from his low-riding 501s. I stroke his length firmly a few times and Danny grabs me tightly around the waist pulling me to his kiss, no longer willing to wait for me. His cock hard, he moves and rubs it against my crotch. My tongue duels with his, in and out of his mouth. Both of us want to move on to the main event. When I wrap my fingers around him, I find I can't reach all the way around, I slide down to investigate the goods. Let's just say he's a tiger, in fact I'll be calling his dick Tiger from now on. I kiss his tip and he shivers at the contact. I take his tip in my mouth, licking and sucking it like a lollipop while I lightly stroke him using both hands. He's at least seven inches in length and he's not fully engorged. He wasn't kidding on the phone, he can do it all—and I want him to.

"Fuck this!" Danny yells out. "I need to have you." He pulls away and grabs me by the hand, pulling my shirt off over my head. Moving quickly to my pants, he unbuttons my jeans and lowers the zipper, pushing them down until they meet the top of my boots. I work my feet together to slide off my boots and my jeans disappear, flung somewhere in the room. I'm left in my matching black lace panties and bra. "This will do, just like this. You're fuckin' hot. Black lace just for me," he mumbles. His hands are immediately on my breasts, and his mouth sucking and licking at my nipple through the lace. His hand finds my panties and he cups me finding out I'm dripping wet for him. He slides his finger along the edge of my panties, teasing me for what feels like forever while he moves the delicate lace material of my bra, freeing my nipple and drawing a whimper from me with his actions. He returns his mouth to mine, kissing me deeply and as if I'm his prized possession. Danny has taken control and he's kissing me mindless. Then all of a sudden he's sliding a finger across my heat and in. My body, on high alert, has reached a new level. He slides his finger in and out while he kisses me and adds a second finger, then a third while he whispers in my ear, "You need to be ready for me, baby. You're so tight. You're going to feel like a virgin to me." He bites at my neck, sucking at the sensitive spot and driving me wild. I miss his hands from my body, but then he's right back kissing me deeply. His hand back at my sex, caressing my mound and sensitive nub, until I buck at him and he shoves his huge hard cock into me in one quick motion causing me to scream out in pleasure. Danny is fucking amazing. "Yeah, baby. You're perfect, even better than I imagined." Danny's eyes close when he strokes into me. He focuses on me, watching me closely while he takes me. I don't speak, I'm along for the ride and he's driving. He keeps studying our connection, watching himself slide in and out. He lies on me and whispers in my ear, "You drive me crazy. This is all I want. I just want to be in you and I have a few more inches to get into you. I can't hold back anymore." He pushes in farther with each pass, stretching me until I have all of him and I can grind against him. I meet his strokes halfway, letting him know I want more. I want everything he has to give.

I don't want him to hold back, "Is that all you've got,

Tiger?" He slams into me, repeatedly hitting my sweet spot and sending me spiraling in an instant.

"Oh. Oh. Jackie. Fuck." My tight wet heat pulls him over the edge with me. He lets out a guttural growl, filling me with satisfaction. He pounds into me repeatedly while he comes and I can feel Tiger pulsating hard. Danny presses on my sensitive nub while he slides in and out, riding out his orgasm. When he finally pulls out he says, "You deserve an extra prize," and without skipping a beat he continues to work my clit as he drops to worship my sex, burying his face in my wetness and sending me to outer space with his tongue. The presence and then absence of Tiger impacts the intensity of my pleasure. Much stronger and more dramatic, uncontrolled release. Freaking amazing. "Ready for round two?" Danny asks. I check the scoreboard, Danny 1, Jackie 3. Danny can have anything he wants and right now he wants me to ride Tiger. Danny sits up with his back against the headboard and pulls me to him, apologizing and saying, "I'm sorry, baby. Round two will be better." I try to figure out how it could be better and why he's apologizing. I kiss him and he's emotionally involved now when he puts his hands on my hips and slides me down on top of Tiger while we kiss. I squeeze him and grind against him. I guess he meant he'd last longer in round two, which may be true, but he's more present and wanting everything, not set on needing to get off. Not that I'm complaining, Tiger is amazing. The full package and less nerves, the electrical fire burning, and connecting his lips on mine to his cock inside me, his intentions, his desire. Danny's chocolate eyes melting me into whatever he wants. I'm in trouble big time and he doesn't know I'm not British. I need to tell him soon. But he pushes into me deeper and plays with my breasts making my mind go absolutely blank of everything except the pleasure of him.

CHAPTER SEVEN

I wake up and it feels like days later, but it's only midnight and someone is knocking on the door. Danny's movement is what woke me, my body is no longer warm and content with him wrapped around me. He answers the door and it's the pizza delivery guy, it smells yummy and makes my stomach rumble. "I ordered dinner. I hope you like pepperoni and sausage with extra cheese. My buddy is delivering tonight, so I had him make a stop for me and pick up a few other things, too. We have sodas, water, ice cream, and Ding Dongs for later. I thought you might want to share some chocolate chip with me for dessert." I smile at him warmly. "This isn't what I had in mind. I wanted to take you out, not bring you to my place and fuck. Okay, I do want to have sex with you until you can't walk, but that was supposed to be later, after we've spent some time together and you know I like hanging out with you. I don't want you to regret me and think I'm using you." He gazes at me sincerely.

"How could anybody ever regret Tiger?" Danny glares at me and I'm filled with regret, I said the wrong thing.

"I'm more than that. I'm more than just my dick!" he says upset.

"Danny, do you think I'd drive here just to get sex? I can get sex without leaving my building." Considering Bryan, Rob, and others I've been turning away. "I can't see you, spend time with you, kiss you and hold onto you. It's stupid, but I missed you and wanted you even though we only spent one night together roaming the strip half drunk."

Danny gets the goofiest smile on his face and I think I'm forgiven for the Tiger comment. I give him a chaste kiss on the lips and go for the pizza. We sit in his bed naked and enjoying each other's company while we destroy the pizza and listen to his boom box that's set on the hard rock station. Apparently, it's all power ballads from 1am until 4am on the weekends—the hard rock version of love songs. The perfect soundtrack to remember my time with Danny. Epic tunes one right after the other, "To Be With You" by Mr. Big, "Love of a Lifetime" by Firehouse, "I'll Be There For You" by Bon Jovi, "Heaven" by Warrant, "I Remember You" by Skid Row, "High Enough" by Damn Yankees, "Home Sweet Home" by Motley Crue and on and on. The pizza was gone and the ice cream was in the freezer. Danny was singing the songs on the radio to me and caressing my arm while he studied me. I should be self-conscious sitting here naked having inhaled a third of a pizza, but I'm not. Something about the way Danny looks at me makes everything okay. He's always happy. He's him and he isn't hiding anything. I hope he doesn't hate me. I start to tell him the truth, but he moves in and kisses me sweetly, playfully, reminding me of our night roaming the strip.

This is the Danny I want. How can I keep him?

He continues to kiss me and holds me close to him, pulling the sheets up over us so we're hiding together in our blanket fort with a hint of a glow from the light in the room shining through. He has the happiness of a child and he gazes at me adoringly. His eyes give him away with the shine and honesty in his features, this is more than a one night stand for him. I snuggle into his chest and he puts his arms around me. There's a sigh of relief from each of us and we fall asleep together.

———

I wake up Saturday morning to the sound of two men talking, a TV on, and a warm man climbing back into bed with me to hold me and kiss my forehead sweetly. I don't know how long Danny's been awake, but I know he isn't naked. I'm naked and Tony's back. I'm comforted by Danny's protection, and I don't have to worry about any of it.

Time for a recap. Danny is amazing and I suck. The end. Okay, that might be a bit too simplified. But, Danny is amazing! In addition to the mind numbing sex and Tiger, he ordered in food without asking and chose perfectly, he kisses me and embraces me like I'm his favorite thing in the world, he's refreshingly playful, and he protects me. Me? Well, I'm a liar taking advantage of this good-hearted, happy-go-lucky, well-hung, beefcake! Granted, I've only lied about being from England, but I've continued the fib with my accent which irritatingly keeps getting better and harder to stop using. Allow me to explain the extent of the British accent problem: I maintained it without a flaw through multiple rounds of Tiger induced orgasms that left me pretty much boneless and dreamy. It might be easier to make my British back-story come true, than to explain myself. If only it would fix everything and make it alright that I may have accidentally started a relationship with the man of my dreams, my soul mate, and king beefcake based on a lie.

What am I thinking? Listen to Jess. He's only a guy in Vegas. Have fun and enjoy yourself, then get away before you get attached. Remember? Exactly what Jess did with Jimmy. He's never going to look at you the same again anyway. Once he finds out you're not British—it's over. I guess there isn't a reason I need to tell him. Why ruin the weekend? Let him have a story to tell his friends about a British chick and absorb every drop of Danny while I can.

Danny pulls the blanket up over his head while I tuck my head into his neck. His voice sweet and caring, he whispers to me, "Good morning, Jacks. May I take you out to breakfast and we can spend some time out together today?" I kiss his chest and run my arm around his neck, playing with the shaggy ends of his hair. "Jacks? Tony is home from work and needs to sleep. Let's get out of here."

I'm screwed. I don't want to give him up! I love the way he's calling me Jacks and what the hell was I thinking giving him my real name? I never give guys my real name. I'm going to stay where I am until he pushes me to get up again.

"Jacks, come on baby. I promise you more later. I want you, too."

I don't have any clothes in reach and I don't want to parade naked in front of Tony. "Okay, but I don't have my clothes."

"Already taken care of, your clothes and your bag are in the bathroom waiting for you with a clean towel. Wrap yourself up in the blanket and walk into the bathroom," Danny has it handled.

"How many times have you done this?" I question since he was so smooth.

"Jacks, I told you I haven't had any other women here. I've

been in your position and done the same thing I'm telling you to do at a girl's house when her roommate got home," he explains quietly.

"I get it. Women love you. Blah, blah, blah," I roll my eyes at him.

"On the East Coast, yeah. Not so much here, and none like you, none ever mattered. Only you, I've never had a girl sleep over at my place," his tone turns serious. "Please get up, we need to get out of here. I want in you and it can't happen. It'll be better this way. Get up. Would you prefer if I take the blanket away, so you have to run to the bathroom nude?" He means it. I get up quickly and go get ready.

I jump in the shower quickly to clean up. I pull on my jeans and a snug fitting Beatles T-shirt, brush my teeth and go outside to brush out my hair. I shove money and ID in my pocket, and grab socks. I put my sneakers on in my truck. I consider what his plan might be for the day. I already messed up Danny's plan for last night. Today, I'm going with the flow and looking forward to the adventure.

I'm sitting in my truck with my feet and legs dangling out the door, pulling my socks and shoes on when Danny walks up. "Breakfast buffet, cheap steak and eggs, or off-strip some-where? You choose."

"Cheap sounds good to me, but I'm not big on steak and eggs. How about cheap pancakes or hash browns?" I suggest hungrily.

"The cheap steak and eggs place happens to have delicious pancakes. Are we walking today or are you driving?"

"Driving. I don't want to wear myself out. I have a feeling it's going to be a late night." I reach both of my arms around his neck and kiss him thoroughly right there in the parking lot. Danny climbs into the passenger side of my truck and directs me to a small old school casino with his hand warm on my thigh.

He grabs my hand and intertwines our fingers for the walk into the casino toward the coffee shop. He doesn't wait to be seated, he walks right in like he owns the place and sits at the counter. A skinny old woman with a beehive hairdo walks up and greets Danny, "Good morning, Sweetcake! I see you've brought a guest with you today." Obviously, Danny's a regular. "What'll you have?"

"I'll take my regular and can you whip up some of your special pancakes for her?" He gives the waitress a big smile.

"You got it, Sweetcake!" She turns to the kitchen and comes right back with a couple of coffees, already prepared with flavored creamer and topped with whipped cream. I take it back, she mixed a packet of hot cocoa mix into the coffee. There's a commotion in the kitchen, apparently the waitress is making my special pancakes. What is this place he brought me to?

"You're going to love this." Danny tells me as he pulls my hand to his mouth and kisses my palm, sending an electrical current throughout my body like a wake-up call. I'm entertained by the place, collections of things everywhere. Not similar to Planet Hollywood or the Hard Rock. No, there are unique collections of kitchen utensils all over the place. Yes, kitchen utensils—graters, juicers, garlic presses, zesters, vegetable peelers, steak knives, soup spoons, can openers, bottle openers, cutting boards, measuring cups—all arranged into pieces of art.

The waitress comes back and drops off Danny's breakfast: steak, eggs, bacon, home fries, white toast with peanut butter, and a bottle of ketchup—enough food for any two people. A minute later she comes back with my special pancakes and they are special. The pancakes are oversized, light and fluffy with chocolate chips in them, a gooey layer of peanut butter melting between the layers, and a banana sliced and placed on top to make it a smiley face. I definitely didn't find this on the menu. Must be a locals thing, or maybe a "Danny's a cutie pie" and the old lady likes him to come eat here thing. I'll probably never find out. The pancakes are perfectly sweet, fluffy, and yummy. I get through about two thirds of them and can't eat anymore, but Danny seems to be a bottomless pit finishing his breakfast for two and my pancakes.

We spend the day walking the strip and taking in the daytime attractions. Including the leftovers from last night who are still roaming the strip in the clothes they went out in and are still partying, drunk, wasted, high, half-naked, or any combination of those things. Las Vegas is a unique place to people watch.

I hate Circus Circus, but with Danny even that mad house was fun. We spent over an hour in the arcade and playing carnival games. Danny pulled me into one of those photo booths and pulled the curtain closed, giving us a few minutes of private time in a crazy place and kissing me silly while he ran the booth taking photos of us. We may have lost the air hockey puck, but whatever.

We hang out in front of Treasure Island for more than 30 minutes, trying to get a good view of the pirate show and it was worth it.

We watch the volcano erupt at the Mirage.

We check out the statues around Caesars Palace, and walk through the Forum Shoppes to watch the lifelike ceiling and live art pieces.

We walk through the car museum at the Imperial Palace.

We relax in the garden at the Flamingo, wandering the paths and looking at all the different birds, from the ducks to the flamingos.

We watch the lions at the MGM, or I should say I watch the lions at the MGM. Danny seems to be focused on something else, me. He has his arms around me from behind, resting his chin on my shoulder while I contently watch the lions. Occasionally he kisses my cheek, which makes me smile uncontrollably. He even whispers sweetly in my ear, "You're so beautiful, Jacks."

The way Danny says "Jacks", it's more than my name or his pet name for me. It's more than him trying to get my attention. It's beyond special. It's only between him and me, and it feels like more. It can't just be my name. It's more than a name, it's almost, dare I say, conveying emotion. It's his voice when he says it, the tone he has tells me everything is the way it's supposed to be and how much he wants me. I knew the first time I heard him call me Jacks, nobody else would ever be the same. Nobody else would ever be my Danny and I would always be the only Jacks.

When we finally get to the Excalibur something is different. Memories of our first kiss fuel our mood. We'd wandered Las Vegas most of the day simply being together and having fun. Getting along, playing, laughing, sharing drinks, and holding hands. It was a day to remember. My cheeks hurt from smiling and laughing. There's a personal connection building between us and it has us trying to get closer to each other. Danny leads me to one of the secluded areas we had found the week before, hoping for a place private enough to make out without getting kicked out. Unfortunately, it's still daytime. There are no areas with dimmed lights, people are everywhere and the casinos are completely open, no closed sections. There's nowhere we can go to just be together and kiss and, okay fine, grope like maniacs who can't keep their hands off each other.

I beam at him with a gleam in my eye and lead him back to

my truck. It's a gorgeous day outside, why not take advantage of it? I ask Danny where there's a park with trees and he stares at me funny, but directs me to one near his room. I find a shaded parking space at the end of the lot, away from everything and everybody. A big tree hanging over it with branches that look like they're made to be climbed, as if it was designed by an artist's mind and not nature. Danny leans in to kiss me and has his hands on me before I can get the emergency brake set. His caress makes me want to stay where I am and let him do whatever he wants. There's no doubt I'll enjoy it. But, he'll appreciate my idea and I don't want to get arrested for public nudity today. "Let's move this party," I tell Danny with a smile and we get out of the truck. I grab my blanket, emergency bag, and snack stash from behind the seat, tossing them into the back of the truck. I arrange the blanket to cover most of the truck bed while still folded in two. I take my beach towel and hoodie from my emergency bag and make them into pillows to lean against. I get comfortable, kick off my shoes and invite Danny to join me as I break into my snack stash of potato chips, cheese and crackers, water, and Peanut M&M's. I'm not actually interested in the snacks, but it seems appropriate to be a picnic. He sits down next to me and I immediately lean into him, reach my arms around him, and press my lips to his greedily. I run my fingers through the shaggy hair at his neck and he releases a groan into my mouth. He pulls me down into the truck bed where we can be alone and we lie there facing each other for the next couple of hours, simply being, talking and gazing into each other's eyes. Not falling. No, absolutely not falling. Never falling, especially not for this easy, uncomplicated man who will be out of my life soon and not ever want to see my face again. Reminder: Do Not Fall. As if I have any control over it.

Danny checks his watch, "Tony should be getting ready and

leaving soon. Do you want to go out dancing or out to dinner or stay in tonight?"

"We've been out all day. I'm fine with picking up take-out and staying in, but whatever you want will work unless you're planning on ditching me somewhere." I gaze at him with a joking grin. He isn't going to leave me alone.

Danny focuses on me with flames burning in his eyes, "You know what I want." My body squeals internally, doing cartwheels and backflips. Danny tries to shake off his sexual desire, "We had pizza last night. There's a diner that makes burgers and designer fries. We can stop and eat, or pick up to go. What do you think?"

"Sounds great. I'm a sucker for french fries."

Danny pulls me against him one last time in the bed of the truck and kisses me, holding me to him, not wanting to stop.

The sun is setting and the sky is changing from clear bright blue to desert hazed with orange and purple hues.

We pack up the picnic and put it away behind the seat where it belongs. It's getting dark out when we get settled into my truck and I turn on the radio, setting the channel to the hard rock station we were listening to last night. "Don't Close Your Eyes" by Kix is playing. The plan is to go to the diner, but one glance at him and I can't help myself. I crawl over to his side of the truck and straddle him with one knee on either side of him, claiming his mouth passionately. He wraps his left arm around my waist, pulling me tight against him. His right hand digs into my hair, grasping it tight while he holds me where he wants me and takes over the kiss. His kiss is soft and sweet unlike his possessive grip on me. He pulls my lips away from his and I find myself reaching back for more. He searches my eyes, his glazed and dark. I watch the smile break across his lips. Both of his hands are immediately on my face, pulling my lips to his.

He tugs at my lower lip and licks across my upper. I open my mouth releasing a sexy sigh and grind against him, out of control and needy. I reach for his fly, wondering if he's going commando again, and give Tiger a rub. I push off my jeans and he immediately slides his finger along the edge of my panties. "Fuck, you're wet for me." I start to unbutton his jeans, my breath ragged with desire and he stops me. "Don't have a condom. Can't do it, Jacks." He's trying to protect us, but it's only words. He wants me, even though we both know better. I'm no tease.

"We won't do it. Just feel it, our connection." It sounds stupid when it comes out of my mouth. Maybe worse than "only the tip" or "I'm married, but a blow job isn't sex, right?"

Danny stares at me, his face telling me it's a bad idea, but his "we shouldn't do this" expression drifted away when I mounted his hard cock right there in my truck. His hands are on my hips while I take some time to get him all the way in, stretching around him and sinking down on him further and further as my body will allow it. Kissing him the whole time and balancing myself with my hands on his shoulders. Without doing anything he tickles my sweet spot and drives me to ride him. I start to move and he stops me quickly. "Don't do it. I can't help myself. I want you too much. I won't stop. I won't pull out. Damn it! You could almost do nothing and I'd go off right now." Danny holds me tightly and doesn't allow me to move. He takes a few deep breaths. "Remember this. I want you to tell me how I feel and how I make you feel, but not until we get to my room."

"I don't have to remember. We'll be doing it again," I stare directly at him with clear intent.

"Yes, we will, Jacks. There will be a condom then and I want you to tell me the difference. Now that I've been bare, I may not want to use a condom again. Feeling you, Jacks—I need more." Danny tries to calm down and regain control.

I reach down and explore our bare connection, aware of how big he is and all I want to do is come. The extreme sensitivity of my nerve center is increased by stretching to accommodate Tiger and I can't help myself. A touch quickly turns to a press, then a rub, and I'm on the edge.

"Jacks, Jacks, Jacks! Stop!" I can't stop and it's intense. I'm squeezing Tiger hard as my orgasm rolls on and on. Danny grabs me on each side and lifts me up and off of him quickly, trying to maintain himself and not go along with my bad idea? Bad manners? Deviant behavior? Life changing risk. Crap. What has gotten into me? Use your brain, Jackie.

"Sorry, um, momentary lapse of brain function. I'm glad your brain is still functioning. Let me make it up to you." I kneel at his feet and stroke him with both hands while I suck and lick at his tip. It won't take long, he's already worked up. I suck on him hard and he starts to come while he watches me. He comes in my mouth and I suck on him like my favorite candy treat until he's finished.

Danny's sated, leaning back in the seat with his eyes closed. I pull his T-shirt down to cover his goods, pull my jeans on, and climb up onto the bench seat next to him, laying my head on his shoulder and my hand on his thigh. Without opening his eyes, he takes my hand in his and leans his head on mine. We sit there together, quiet as the sky grows dark, and it's perfect.

CHAPTER EIGHT

I need to get my head straight. I mean, any red-blooded woman would be a fool not to enjoy Tiger's company. The problem is Danny. And the fact that Tiger is only a small part of Danny. Well, maybe not a small part, but you know what I mean. His smile and warm eyes make me happy all over. His hands light my skin on fire, yet somehow comfort me at the same time. My heart is what I'm worried about. My heart needs to stay out of this. It's bad enough I need to get better control of my body, and I can't beat Tiger in that competition. Tiger will win out every single time. Yeah, my head definitely needs to be strong and take control of all my other parts. No more doing anything stupid, no matter how fucking amazing it is. No more enjoying the closeness. This is fun. This is just sex. Okay, this is great sex. Who am I kidding? This is unbelievably hot fucking attraction and I want more! Where is my head when I need it and why won't it beat my body into submission? Please brain, at least take control of my heart.

Danny stares at my face, "What are you thinking? Are you okay in there?"

"Nothing." Crap. Quick thinking, Jackie. Not! There's no way he takes that answer.

"More like something, there's always something going on in there." He sits, waiting for an answer.

Get it together, Jackie. Make it good. "Um, I, uh, I apologize about earlier. I've never lost control and gone bare before. I'm not sure what came over me. You must have turbo pheromones or something. Definitely a chemical reaction. Anyway, it won't happen again. I have better control than that." Much better than "you make me lose control and I want to keep you, but I can't because you're going to hate me tomorrow."

Danny shows me his frown for the first time, "I kind of like it when you lose control."

I don't want to see that face on him, he needs to smile. "I'll still lose control for you, just not the crazy way."

"I know it's bad, but I kind of like the crazy way. Maybe you make me crazy, too. I want you, Jacks. I want all of you." Using his I-mean-it tone and giving me chills throughout my body.

"I get it, Danny. I totally get it. I," I take a deep breath and continue, "I can't go there. I'm leaving tomorrow. I may never see you again." I listen to the sadness in my voice, aware of the truth—it will be over.

"I promise you'll see me again. There's more to us than this weekend." Danny presses his lips to mine softly and sweetly, then pulls back and gazes into my eyes. I hope he sees me and not my lie. I'm afraid to dive too far into his eyes, not sure of what I'll find there. "Let's go back to my place, Jacks. I've got plans for us."

I drive the few blocks to his room and Tony's already gone. He left a note saying he's hoping to stay at a friend's after work and we know it's code for he has a girl lined up. We also know we have the place to ourselves until our weekend is over. I don't like the word over.

"Jacks, how about we call in an order to the diner? We can walk over to pick it up." Danny suggests.

"Whatever you want. I'm fine sharing the ice cream with you for dinner."

Danny gazes at me, appreciating the "whatever he wants" part of the statement. "That would be great, but we need energy," he says with a dirty wiggle of his eyebrows. "You said whatever I want. I know what I want," his voice getting softer.

I belly laugh at him and he grins as he picks up the phone to place an order with the diner. "Ready in 30 minutes." He grabs me, "What can I do in 30 minutes and still have time to walk to the diner?" He kisses me firmly and works my jeans off completely, giving them a toss to the other side of the room. Danny slides his hands down my body until he's on his knees and pushes my feet apart, spreading my legs. He kisses my lace panties and slides them to the side with his finger, teasing me with the light touch of his fingers on my sex. He presses his lips to my upper thigh, then my clit, then my wet heat, and settles in with his tongue lapping at me luxuriously. Sucking and nibbling at my folds, working his tongue in deep and making low noises of satisfaction that vibrate through me.

My body belongs to him, no wonder my brain can't control it. I find myself waiting for him to breathe, hanging on his every move, wanting more. He must sense it, moving his mouth to my sensitive nub and sucking hard as he slides a finger in and curls it to touch a magical place. I scream out, "Danny, Danny, Oh Danny!" and he searches my eyes with need as he slides into me bare.

Stroking very slowly, he whispers in my ear, "Jacks baby, don't worry. I'll never hurt you. I won't come. I promise. I, I need to feel you my way. You're amazing." Danny presses his lips to my neck slightly below my ear, tenderly kissing and tasting me. His heart is beating strong. His hands are moving and he gently rubs my center to draw out another orgasm, sending me over the edge with hardly any effort. After a few minutes, he pulls out of me and I feel like something's missing without him. I reach for him and he pulls me up to him, holding me tight. "Why don't you stay here and relax, while I pick up? I'll be less than 15 minutes."

Since I'm completely boneless and lacking brain function, I nod in agreement. Danny smiles at me, gives me a kiss and says, "We'll finish this when I get back," as he runs out the door.

———

First, I'm having trouble speaking at the moment. Everything is in my head and even that is in a British accent. Fuck me. Second, how does he keep getting better? I need one of my girls to bring me back to my senses. Jess doesn't know I'm in Vegas and would spend the amount of time I have for the call berating me. Dot will most likely encourage my actions, but she can be a pillar of common sense and she's what I need right now.

I find my pants and get some change from my truck ashtray on my way to the pay phone. I dial up Dot, hoping she answers and I didn't waste the change I had on her husband or her answering machine.

"Hello?"

"Hey Dot, I'm checking in with you from Vegas," trying to stay upbeat and not show my current state.

"I was wondering about you. Are you having fun? Any sex? Tell me about the package," typical Dot.

"I'm fine. I'm having fun and I'll meet you for lunch this week to tell you all about the rest. Um, I only have a few minutes and I need someone who still has their wits about them."

"That doesn't sound good. Why are you using the British accent? You didn't tell him. And, let me guess... He's amazing in the sack, fun, and you like him and his hot bod?" nail meet head.

"Sounds right, but you're underestimating his package, his tongue skills, his fucking hot body, the way his tiger tattoo drives me crazy, and the way he looks at me. The sweet things he says to me. He's real, Dot. He's not full of shit."

"That's great. Oh, that's not good," I can tell Dot doesn't have a clue where to go with this. "Look girl, don't freak out. Enjoy the rest of your weekend and have fun. See what happens. I'd tell you to hide your heart, but I have an idea it's already too late for that. Or, come home now. I've got your back either way chickadee."

At least she's thinking the same way I am. I'm not crazy. "Thank you. We need to get together tomorrow night or Monday. Send me the code and let me know when. I'll call when I'm leaving tomorrow." I hang up and go back to the room to find I've locked myself out.

Quick recap: It's dark. I'm in the not so nice and not so clean part of Vegas, just off the strip. I'm barefoot. I'm standing in front of a locked door at a no-tell motel and I don't have a key. I can sit here on the window ledge like a hooker waiting to turn a trick, hoping my pimp doesn't catch me taking a break or I can go out into the parking lot and sit in my truck. If I go sit in my truck, Danny might think I'm leaving. Neither option is acceptable, or safe. Then again, I haven't been playing it safe today.

Danny walks around the corner with his arms full and stares at me quizzically. I rush to meet him and help him carry. He has more than an order from the diner, unless he ordered for three people again. "I was looking forward to coming back and finding you the way I left you. What are you doing outside?"

"I needed to call and check in." I shake my head at myself, still in denial. "I went to use the payphone and locked myself out," berating myself internally.

"You ran across a parking lot in Las Vegas barefoot?" he glares at me questioning my judgment.

"Twice," I reply quickly. "I probably look like a hooker waiting for my John to show up."

Danny laughed, "So, Jess keeps tabs on you or only because it's me?"

"I didn't tell Jess I was going to Vegas. Dot, however, is simply concerned I might get stuck somewhere and wants to make sure she doesn't need to call out the hounds. She also wants to live vicariously through my exploits."

"I'm happy somebody is looking out for you. I don't want anything to happen to you." Danny says sincerely as he unlocks the door.

I immediately take my jeans off and help him with the food. It smells delicious and I had no idea how hungry I was. He has a giant order of waffle fries with grated cheese melted on them, topped with pulled pork and a bunch of containers with extra stuff to add on top, including green onions, red onions, salsa, sour cream, jalapeños, and cheese sauce. There's a big bacon cheeseburger and a huge chocolate milkshake. Danny also picked up some Sprite and Midori, which he puts in the refrigerator to chill.

Danny hits the power on his boom box and turns to me, "I like that you're back to no pants," with a sexy grin on his face.

"I set the standards for tonight already. I told you it's whatever you want. You said you were looking forward to coming back and finding me how you left me—I was without pants."

He takes his shirt off and we sit Indian-style on his bed sharing the fries. I begin to feed him and if I get anything on him, I lick it off. Salsa on his chest, I lick it off. Cheese sauce on his lip, I suck it off. When my fingers get close to his mouth, he sucks them into his mouth and pulls me close making a mess of everything, but most importantly he makes me smile and laugh.

We spend the evening snuggling together in bed watching movies and listening to music. Well, it was all going on in the background and around us while we enjoyed being together. I've never been this comfortable and at ease with any man. Playfully reaching for each other and exploring each other, because there'd be no objection. Simply being together and enjoying the company. Unable to keep our hands to ourselves. Kissing me into whisker burn and not even caring. Lying together and getting lost in each other's eyes. Heated moments driving our desire for connection. Hearts racing and unable to stop ourselves once we start, passion and need taking over, everything out of our control.

Danny's eyes go dark and hooded. "I need you, Jacks. I need to have you." He whispers in my ear as he pushes into me. "How are you so perfect?" Stroking in and out slowly, going deeper every time while he buries Tiger inside me. I moan at his motions. "You drive me crazy with your cries." He gets all the way in and continues slowly, deliberately, sliding in and pulling out. His hot breath at my ear unsteady with every stroke. His hands in my hair, holding himself up with his elbows.

"Danny, more please. More," I urge him from the edge of sanity.

"No, Jacks. I want this to last." Unwavering. "Remember, you said 'whatever I want.'"

"Yes. Whatever you want. You're unbelievable." I meant it when I said it. I'd do anything for this man.

"Jacks, tell me how I feel. Tell me how I make you feel," Danny says concentrating and barely able to speak.

"You push me to my limits and make me ready to explode. Completely filled and stretched exquisitely, like no one else could do. It's you, Danny. Tiger is you and it wouldn't matter what size you are, you'd still make me feel this way." I listen to the words come out of my mouth at the same time Danny hears them. Simply honest words, and my heart clenches at how much trouble I'm in. It's stupid, but I don't want to leave him and I'll be driving home to my real world tomorrow, leaving him behind.

Inspired by my words, he gazes deeply into my eyes and presses his lips to mine. His kiss is full of intent and different than any he has given me before. What this man lacks in vocabulary and intelligence are conveyed in his actions, made up for with his honesty and his heart. With Danny, what you see, feel, hear—him... is what you get. "I wish you could stay with me. I know that's not going to happen. Maybe someday," he whispers quietly. I'm not sure he meant to say it out loud. We're thinking the same thing and wanting the same thing. It's an unbelievably fantastic feeling and it makes me feel like crap, but I'm going to forget about it. I'm blocking it out until I get home. I'm having this Danny time.

The heat and friction is building between us, even at his slow pace. "Jacks, I'm going to make you go off harder than you ever have. I want to feel your orgasm around me. Then I'm going to pull out. Where do you want me to come?" He's up on his knees with his eyes closed, talking to me and squeezing my breasts.

I wasn't aware we weren't using a condom and the risk adds to my excitement. "It's whatever you want tonight. That's not changing."

"Oh, yeah." He says as he strokes into me deep hitting my magic spot repeatedly and he circles my sensitive nub with growing intensity.

I scream out his name over and over and over, hearing it and not comprehending it's me begging him for more—it's me needing him. "Harder, Danny. Please. More!" I call out uncontrollably and this time he does what I request, pounding into me hard and I explode. Everything goes dark. All I can see is bright explosions in my eyes when I dive over the edge head first into a spiraling orgasm, grasping for any part of him I can reach.

Danny is out of his mind, "No, not yet, not yet, not yet. I want more. I'm not pulling out yet. I want to feel more. You're so fucking amazing around me." He pounds into me fast and hard, pulling out suddenly. I move quickly and kiss him passionately, sucking on his tongue while he pulls the last few strokes of his orgasm.

We collapse on the bed, both of us out of breath and silent. He reaches for me and brings my naked body to his, holding me snug against him. Pressing his lips to any part of me in his reach, in a cherishing way. His heart is still beating hard and he hasn't caught his breath yet. My heart is beating as hard as his and his hand is over my heart, taking comfort in it's beat. No words pass between us, they aren't needed to express where we are. We're happy right now. We don't want to be brought down by tomorrow. We don't want it to be over. I don't like the word over.

It's after 1am because the radio changed to power ballads, but I didn't notice it until Danny started singing one of the songs to me. Foreigner is playing "Waiting For a Girl Like You" and the first words out of either one of us is Danny singing the chorus. He's smiling against my skin, singing the words into my ear quietly. He keeps going with the next verse. He doesn't sing the last two lines of the verse, the part with the L word—when you love someone—he simply kisses my neck. It may have made it worse because he kept it to himself and didn't say the words, it's obvious he's familiar with the words. The reaction of his body against mine tells me the truth of it caught him off guard. He was trying to be sweet and had an epiphany, probably not what he was planning on. Then again, I'm sure I'm not at all what he was planning on. He had no idea we'd be in this place. This weekend hasn't been at all what I anticipated. It's been much better, yet crappy and scary at the same time. I wouldn't change it for anything. I shouldn't analyze everything, maybe he was done singing. I shouldn't be surprised, I'm careful to never use the L word.

Danny's arms around me are warm, strong, and protective, he's my own private security system. My guard is down and I'm relaxed because of him. He won't let anything happen to me. I lay my head on his chest and listen to his heartbeat, tracing his tiger tattoo aimlessly until I fall asleep.

CHAPTER NINE

I wake up the next morning with my head tucked into Danny's chest. He's holding me close and the blankets have been pulled up over our heads. The radio is playing all Beatles. Makes sense, its Sunday morning and the LA station plays Breakfast with the Beatles every Sunday. Part of me wants to run. Get out and be gone without having to talk to him—avoid any possible emotional departure. Part of me wants to stay right where I am and not move a muscle, absorbing every last drop of Danny I can while not disturbing him. It's risky. I do have to leave today. I have work tomorrow morning and traffic driving from Las Vegas to LA on Sunday sucks. I have no idea what time it is, but I bet it's early enough I could hit the road and avoid the never-ending sea of cars. Otherwise, I need to wait until the early evening and it'll still take at least four hours to get home.

Here's the problem: There's absolutely no way I make it through this day without thinking about leaving and getting sad, because I'm never coming back to this. I did this to myself. I need to set this weekend and Danny free. Pretend the whole thing didn't happen and he doesn't exist. Or, tell him I'm not British, so he can start to hate me. I don't want to do either one. How am I supposed to forget him? I'm going to ignore all of this drama and suck it up. Maybe he won't page me again, ever. Still, it doesn't solve my problem, when do I leave? Not until I have to.

"Jacks, baby? Are you awake?" Danny whispers into my hair. I snuggle into him and kiss his chest. "My sweet, sticky, Jacks… we need to shower."

"I'm fine right here," I talk into his chest and find his nipple to tease. Danny releases a deep sigh and throws the blankets off. He sits up, taking me with him into his lap and kisses my forehead while he cradles me. He somehow manages to get to the edge of the bed and stand up with me in his arms. He carries me with him effortlessly, like I'm nothing, and that's not the case. He's stronger than I anticipated and I'm starting to get the idea showering may be for more than getting clean. Was I going to leave before morning sex? I must be a crazy girl!

Danny gives me instructions, "I'm going to set you down on your feet, turn on the shower and step into the other room to give you a minute to do whatever you need to do without me in the room. Then it's shower time." My feet hit the ground and he leaves the room, closing the door behind him. This is the first time I've stood since I locked myself out yesterday. Lots has happened since then. Let's just say he wasn't kidding when he said he was going to fuck me until I couldn't walk. Funny thing, I'm anxious for more.

Danny comes back with a twisted expression, "Why are you leaning on the wall?"

"Honest?"

"Yes, Jacks."

"Walking and standing are a slight challenge," sheepishly and hoping he'll help.

"Are you okay? Oh. Maybe I can help." He picks me up and takes me into the shower with him, but he doesn't set me back down on the ground. I'm pinned between his body and the wall with the warm water falling on us and his hands all over me. He kisses my neck and scrapes his teeth across the sensitive skin. Tiger is reaching for me, bumping against me with need. Danny is gorgeous with his wet hair falling straggly into his face and around his neck. The light reflects off his wet body, accentuating his muscles. The tip of his tongue sticks out, teasing me and I take the bait, kissing him full on with an open-mouth, my tongue rubbing and sucking on his until I've got him groaning.

"Baby, tell me you brought a condom in here with you." He's at my entrance and I want him inside me.

"I have a better idea," as he slides me down his body and onto Tiger, maneuvering his way in until he's completely seated inside me.

"Danny, we can't keep…" and I'm lost by his motion in me, against me, his hands. It's all too much for me at once. I whimper uncontrollably and hold on tight for the ride, digging my fingers into his shoulders with my head tilted back and leaning on the shower wall. He takes advantage of my exposed neck, licking and biting softly, kissing my collarbone and below my ear. "Oh, Danny! Baby, you're the best. So fucking perfect." I scream out, calling his name and making noises I've never heard before as he pulls me away from the wall with my legs wrapped around him and takes me to the bed. He sits down on the edge of the bed with me on him, both of us dripping wet and it doesn't matter.

He leans back on the bed and guides my hips to ride him. "That's it, Jacks. Just like that. Don't worry, I'm under control.

We're getting you off first." He gets me into the pattern he wants and continuing without his guidance, then he starts talking to distract me from other things. "Jacks, you're so tight around me. I look at the size of my cock compared to you and I don't understand how you can take me all the way like this. You make me so hard. You look and feel beautiful." His hands are at my sex as he fills me and teases my clit. "Baby, we need to do this right," he says lifting me off of him and getting a condom. Standing at the foot of the bed, he calls me over to him with Tiger straight out at full attention. He turns my back to him and pulls me against him, Tiger between my legs trying to get in. He bites at my neck and whispers, "Bend over, Jacks." He slides into me from behind and pounds away, harder than any other time. He starts slow and gradually gets faster. Holding me at my hips and using my body against his. Moving me, pulling me to him and pushing me away. "You're so wet." He stops and drops to his knees needing to taste me, licking and sucking at my sex aggressively. I start to go over the edge, "No, not yet." He's immediately back to his feet and sliding into me. I hear him call out in pleasure as he reconnects with me. "We're going together this time, Jacks." He reaches for my sensitive center, rubbing in time with his strokes. I'm all raw nerves on end. Every touch is intensified. I reach back to find his cock sliding in and out of me, dragging my finger along his vein. I slam back into him meeting him half way and he's on the edge. He grabs my hips and pulls me back against him hard, once, twice, three times and I'm lost over the edge as he pulsates inside me. When he pulls out, he rolls me over and drops to his knees burying his face in my sex until he has sent me to oblivion again, and again.

Future Reference: If a man doesn't treat me right, they don't get to have me and I'm kicking them out. If I use Danny as the standard, treating me right means I get off three times as often as they do, and first. They should want to hold me and be close to me, even after sex. Nobody gets me without a condom.

I'm not sure what to do and I don't want to talk. The end is getting closer with every second that passes and I don't trust myself. I wait for Danny's lead, but he disappears into the bathroom long enough for mc to get my things together and decide what clothes to put on. Yes, I'm considering the possibility of ditching while he's in the bathroom. I'm moving frantically, getting ready and leaving the actual putting on of the clothes until the last thing. It's a chicken shit thing to do, but I'm not sure what I'm more scared of—my loose lips sinking the ship, spending the rest of my days using a British accent being Mrs. Danny, leaving and never seeing Danny again, or crying. I hate showing my tears.

Danny walks out of the bathroom with a towel wrapped around his waist and his hair dripping wet. He notices my bag, "Are you leaving?"

"I don't want to be in the way. Thank you for inviting me to visit and stay with you. I was starting to get my things together and considering clothing for the day." I keep it factual and keep my emotions in check.

"Jacks, are you kidding me? You're not in the way." Danny walks up to me and puts his hands on my arms.

"You have to go to work and I have to drive back to LA, so I can work tomorrow. Tony will be back and not want to find me here. The weekend has been wonderful."

"Jacks? What happened when I went into the bathroom? Where'd my playful Jacks go?" Searching me, trying to figure out what happened, but he can't see it because it's all in my head. Well, unless you count the knot in my stomach and my heart breaking into pieces.

"Nothing happened. The real world has to continue. We

don't get to hide under the blankets and pretend we're enjoying a weekend together forever." I'm trying my best to hold it together. He doesn't need to learn how close I am to tears.

"Why do you want to leave right now? At least let me make my case…" Danny presses his lips to mine tenderly, swiping his tongue across my lips and parting them to tango with my tongue. And I mean tango, it was a sensual dance and he's not letting me go. I get weak in my knees. "I don't know a better way to let you know what I think and what I want. I'm better with actions than words." Then he goes back to kissing me, squeezing me tight with his arms wrapped around me. Danny pulls back and focuses on me, then leans in to whisper in my ear, "You don't need to cry, Jacks. I don't want you to leave. We need time. We'll figure this out. This is just the beginning." I taste the tears in my mouth and he must've, too.

"You should know, I'm a thief. I'm taking the Ramone's T-shirt you wore yesterday." I tell him trying to break my mood.

"You can take a clean shirt, you don't need to take a dirty one."

"I want the dirty one because it smells like you," I snatch it off the bed and pull it on over my head, enjoying his scent as it surrounds me.

"More important than my shirt, you're stealing a piece of my heart. I'll miss you, Jacks. Are you giving me any more of your time today or are you leaving?" Danny kisses my cheek, then my neck, then nibbles on my earlobe. He runs his fingers through my hair. He makes it extremely obvious he wants all of my time.

He wants to see me again. He says it's just the beginning. He says I'm taking a piece of his heart. He's going to miss me. He doesn't even know who I am.

Apparently, I hesitate too long and defaulted to Danny gets

what he wants. I'm not complaining. I don't want to make any decisions today. He gently and tenderly kisses me, sucking lightly and pulling on each of my lips repeatedly. His hands hold me and move me to where he wants me, he's completely in control. He uses his hands on my breasts, sensually rubbing and squeezing them while he pushes me back down onto the bed. He climbs up over me and one at a time he takes my breasts into his mouth, tracing them with his tongue. He lays on me, naked between my legs and he continues to play with my breasts. His weight against me, his actions at my chest, and his fresh man scent work together at my senses, making me want him. He's making me hot from the inside out. Men don't make me hot like this, only him. He deciphered the secret code or he has the map to the buried treasure. No, that's not it at all. He's simply the prince with the magical kiss that awakens Sleeping Beauty, and his kiss is magical. He makes me forget everything and live in the moment. He gets annoyed with his towel and tosses it away. He moves to claim my mouth and his hips move against me. "I don't know why I can't control myself around you. I always want you. It's never like this. I don't bring chicks home and if I go to their place, I hit it and they never hear from me again. But with you? All I can think about is how I want more and when will I get to have you again."

"It's because I have to go home and you don't have to see me again. You don't have to worry about running into me accidentally on the street or anything after I'm gone. I don't provide a permanent threat. We always want what isn't available." I explain the psychology of it.

"Stop!" He sighs in frustration. "Damn it, Jacks! I want you to be available." He kisses me wildly, stroking my tongue with his. "I can't stand that you're going home and other guys will be there trying to get you, and touch you the way I do. I want you to remember me every minute. I'm going to make sure you can't forget me." Danny reaches for a condom and caresses my wet folds with his fingers, sliding one in while he tongues my sensitive nerve center. I arch into it and he slides a second finger in. I moan out his name and it drives him further. He moves back up to my breasts and Tiger is at my entrance again. He moves higher up my body where he whispers in my ear, "I'm better with actions than words, so I'm going to tell you what I'm doing and I'm doing this because I want you to come back to me. I feel your entrance at the tip of my cock and we want in. I'm pushing in until you're full. I'm feeling you around me tight while I push in and pull out of you and your hot wet body. I'm working my way all the way in, so I can reach your sweet spot. I like to see your face when I hit the spot over and over, it makes me happy to give you pleasure. I'm almost there. Here I come, going to hit the spot. Yeah, that's right. There's the face I was working for and the sexy whimpers. My reward is your pleasure. Your whimpers drive me to do more, to touch you, lick you, kiss you, suck on you, or like now, just fucking use my rock solid shaft to drive into you harder and faster. That's it, the needy cry I like to hear from your lips, the one asking for even more, the one calling out my name telling me I'm your world in that moment. You need to remember that moment when I'm your world. Right baby, you're right there and calling out my name. I don't even think you know when you do it. You make me feel like you're here for my pleasure, to do what I want. But the truth is, I'm here only for you and your pleasure is where mine comes from. I'm coming in harder soon, pounding that spot of yours that makes you scream out uncontrollably and tell me all kinds of things that blow up my ego. You make me feel like a rock star."

I'm listening to the neighbors having sex or a movie on

skinamax, but it's my voice, "Danny, don't stop. Don't stop. Please. Oh my god. Please don't stop. Oh. More. Please, oh Danny. Danny! Danny! Danny! You're the master! Fucking amazing! Don't stop!"

"I can feel how close you are baby. I'm not stopping. You're so wet. I'm going harder, are you ready?" I nod silently wanting whatever he'll give me. "I'm going to slam into you like crazy, one, two, oh fuck this is amazing. Tell me if I hurt you. I don't want to hurt you, baby." Danny loses ability to speak and he continues to slam into me harder and harder and harder with growing speed. We both suddenly scream out at the same time and he wraps his arms around me tightly, not letting me go while he keeps pounding, riding us through the darkness and fireworks. Leaving me unable to move or even comprehend my existence. All I can see is darkness. All I can feel is Danny.

CHAPTER TEN

Hours later we are both awakened suddenly by someone at the door and surprised to find we'd been sleeping. "Tony?" Danny yells out.

"Yeah, it's me," Tony says with a tone of irritation.

"Give me 30 seconds please," Danny yells back and quickly gets up gathering everything he's thrown around the room, then climbs back in bed and pulls the blankets up over us. "Okay, thank you."

The door opens and Tony starts in, "Geez! You stay up all night? How much sex did you need? Looks like you fucked each other's brains out."

Danny pulls the blanket over our heads, "We aren't home. Be out later." I giggle and he can't help but to laugh. He makes me forget everything. He pulls me back against him snugly, with his mouth at my ear, and his hands low on my stomach. Satisfaction in his body.

"It's getting late and I should probably go," I say quietly. "I don't want to, but the real world and all."

"I know, baby. We'll be together again soon. I wish this

could be the real world." He kisses my neck and then my cheek. "I'm going to hold the blanket up, so you can get dressed behind it and Tony will never know the difference." I laugh and go along with it.

I get dressed quickly and I smell like him, I love it. He pulls on his jeans, always going commando. I do a double check to make sure I have all my things in my bag while Danny gets his keys and shoves something in his pocket. He glares at me torn, "I'd carry your bag to your truck for you, but I don't want to make it easier for you to leave."

Tony chimes in, "Don't be a schmuck."

Danny picks up my bag and we walk toward my truck slowly. He has my bag in one hand and he's holding my hand with the other, stroking my wrist with this thumb.

Time for a break, reality check, mental breakdown, whatever. I need to remember the real world. This parting isn't going to go well. I'm going to lose it. It's different for me than it is for him—for him this is the beginning and I'm British, but I'm a California Girl and it's over. I seriously dislike the word over.

"Don't be upset, Jacks. We'll be together again soon. Here, this is for you so you can see me every day." He hands me a photo strip of us making eyes at each other and making out in the photo booth. To be clear, we were in serious make out mode and the machine caught us stopped and gazing at each other like teenagers in love. Teenage love is young and naïve, never real. It's all lust and sexual exploration. The difference is we're in our twenties and neither of us are naïve or sexually inexperienced. This must be all lust and the excitement of somebody new, right? Worse than that for me, could the chance of getting caught in my lie be making this more arousing and exhilarating for me? It doesn't matter. This is all over for me when I drive out of this parking lot. Damn it! I hate the word over.

Danny grabs me when I start to climb into my truck and pulls my body to his. His right hand at the small of my back. His left hand on my neck. Securely holding me where he wants me. He stops before his lips meet mine and reads my eyes like he wants to know everything or maybe he's searching to find out how I feel about him, if I truly want him. I want confirmation when I might fall. Don't even consider it, remember no falling. He kisses me sweetly, tasting and exploring my lips as if he's trying to commit them to memory. He pulls back to gaze at me for the last time and I'm overcome by the view of him shirtless, abs, tiger tattoo, shaggy blonde hair, brown melting eyes, and overall hotness. The fact he's packing Tiger in his button-fly jeans just adds to it. I shiver and Danny gets a big smile as he comes in for the kill, I mean mind-melting kiss. The shiver in my body is all him and he's proud of it. His kiss goes on forever and I can't get enough. His hands hold me as if I'm his, and for the first time, I might be. I break the kiss at the shock of being his, how much I want to be his. Danny stops, still searching me, "Jacks, I am going to see you again. Will you come back for me? I can take the bus to LA. We can get a room somewhere with no Tony." If I answer him I'll be lying or driving back to Las Vegas for more Danny time, because I can't tell him I'm not coming back. I can't tell him I'm a lie. I can't lie to him again. "I am going to see you again, right?" Danny presses to hear the answer from me and his eyes tell me he needs confirmation I'll be back.

"Yes, of course. I can't wait to see you again." Not good, but completely true. It'll be better anyway. I shouldn't leave him wondering and disappear with no closure or reasoning at all. It wouldn't be cool to break it to him over the phone, he might not believe me. Next time I visit him I'll tell him the truth and apologize for leading him to believe I'm something I'm not. Though he has seen the real me in every other way, probably more than anybody else. Any chance the British thing isn't a deal breaker?

I climb into my truck and Danny leans in to whisper in my ear, "You don't belong to me and I'm not asking you to be only mine after the short time we've had together, but when another man wants you, even if it's only for a hug or to hold your hand —remember me, think of me, know I'm waiting for you and how I make you feel. Remember the moment we're together when I'm your world and nothing else exists. I've never had that with anybody else and I'm willing to bet you haven't either." He kisses me again, passionately, telling me without words that he doesn't want me to leave. He steps away without saying goodbye and closes my door. He waves, acknowledging I should go. He's sad and doesn't want me to leave. Tears are already starting to pour down my face.

I don't mind the tears, I don't want anybody else to witness them. I'm a girl, not a robot and my emotions aren't always in check. Windows down, radio blasting, driving fast on the freeway will get me back in control of my life. It'll be late when I get home. I can go straight to bed and not get back in my head. No calling Danny unless he pages me, and he will. I yell at myself internally most of the drive home for not telling him and for all kinds of other things I did or agreed to that I shouldn't have in the last 48 hours. Mostly, I can't stop remembering how he makes me feel and how he has the power to make me forget everything else. Add the "oh my" sexiness and a girl is fuckin' screwed! Probably multiple times.

CHAPTER ELEVEN

I get home to find a note on my door from Rob. He's apologizing for not talking to me for a week, wanting to talk to me, and worried because I haven't returned his calls. I throw it away, like it never existed. Maybe he'll get a clue. I can't even count the number of times I've dumped him, and he always thinks I'm kidding or doesn't take me seriously. First, a boyfriend should take you seriously. Second, if your girl has tried to dump you, it's a stupid idea to not talk to her for a week —you gave her a reward and she's happy you're gone.

I page Dot the code to tell her I'm home, but it's too late to actually call her. I'm sure I'll get a page from her tomorrow.

I lock myself in my apartment and unpack. I go straight to bed because it's late. I can't bear to part with the Ramone's T-shirt, I'll be sleeping in it with its Danny smell—probably for days.

———

About 2:15am there's someone at my door and I do my best to

ignore it. I don't want to get out of bed. I don't want to deal with the real world, leave me to my sweet, incoherent dreams. The knock turns to banging, and I get up to find out who it is before they wake the whole building. I peek through the peephole at Bryan. What the hell? I open the door to, "Why didn't you show up at my gigs this weekend? You were out Friday and Saturday. Your truck wasn't here when I came by."

"Sorry, I was out of town. I just got back a few hours ago."

"You have a new guy? Yeah, you do. I'm looking at his shirt. I bet you weren't 'sick' last week either." He sounds irritated and I'm not in the mood.

"What's up with you, Bryan? You're acting all jealous and we're just friends. Last I checked you have a girlfriend and don't do commitments, but the girlfriends never know that." The words come out harsher than they should've. He woke me up!

"I always know you're here for me and you weren't. Rob was never real for you, he didn't count like you actually had a real boyfriend. But, you haven't even told me about this guy. I don't like it." Bryan acts like he has a say in the matter.

"You don't own me. We're friends. Yes, there's a new guy. I don't know what's going to happen with him and I doubt it's going to last long. So, why don't you leave me to deal with my own drama and let me sleep since I have work in the morning? I'm sure you'll be back to fucking me whenever you want in a few weeks, but you know what? I take it back. You don't deserve me. I deserve to be number one, treated with respect, not woken up at 2am for questioning, and a guy to get me off more than he gets himself off. That's it! I love you, Bryan, and you'll always be my friend. But, my guy will either worship me or get the fuck out. I'm worth more than being sex on the side or sex when you want it." If he didn't wake up the neighbors banging on my door, I did yelling at him.

"What's gotten into you? Sorry I woke you."

"What's got into me? Dude, you need to decide if you're only a friend, or if you want to worship me and only me when my new guy goes bad. I mean it when I say it'll go bad fast. It's my own fault and I wish I could take it back, but I can't and he's…" I stop talking because Bryan doesn't need the details and I don't need to hear myself say it out loud. "Goodnight." I slam the door shut and go back to bed.

CHAPTER TWELVE

Monday morning comes way too early. I wake up with tears running down my face and I look like shit. I go to work and make my Monday morning calls, digging for sales to help stock whatever the stores ran out of over the weekend or whatever all of a sudden is in high demand. I search warehouse locations on some music they played on the hard rock Vegas radio station. I spend a couple of hours in the warehouse filling special orders and searching the stacks for a couple new CDs. I need some Foreigner, Firehouse, maybe Skid Row, and some time alone. This will sound strange because I'm talking about work, but the stacks in the warehouse where I can wander through the records, cassettes, 8-tracks, CDs, simply the history of music ranging from mortifying to legendary is one of my happy places. I'm alone there, except I'm not alone because all of my favorite musicians, the greats, the one hit wonders, the soundtrack to my life—are all there to embrace me. Sometimes I thumb through a shelf I wasn't planning to go to and there's an album beckoning me to pick it up, touch it, read it, research it, and listen to it. Other times, I need comfort and I find myself looking at a CD from a familiar artist featuring the song that will make everything better, or maybe it's the timeframe it's from soothing me—maybe only for me and most likely nobody else would get it, but it gives me the answer I need to continue. Today I'm looking for an answer to comfort me, but it isn't here. Maybe I'm not ready for the answer yet. Makes sense, considering I don't know what the question is. I get back into work mode and ship out my special orders before the cut-off time.

As soon as I step into the office my pager goes crazy, vibrating with four pages. One is Dot from about fifteen minutes ago and she sent me the code for coffee after work. The other three are all 702—Danny, and they came in over the last two and a half hours. Apparently, my pager doesn't work out in the warehouse. I'm not sure about the impatience of three pages. Or, should I take it as a compliment? What if something's wrong? Huh, talk about a quick slide from irritation to worry. The pages did come from two different 702 numbers, interesting. I go to the back office to make a quick phone call and dial the first 702 number, but nobody answers. I try the second 702 number and Danny answers.

"Hello?"

I turn on the British accent and cringe at my continued lie, "Hi, Danny."

Danny sighs in relief, "Jacks, I wanted to make sure you got back to LA safe. I needed to hear your voice and know you're okay." The sound of his voice alone sends my body into high alert and makes my heart pound in my chest.

"You're so sweet. I don't have much time. Can I call you this evening?"

"I work tonight."

"Page me on your break and I'll call you right back, baby."

"It's going to be late. After midnight, maybe 2am. I don't want to wake you up."

"Maybe I want you to wake me up. I'll be in bed, snuggled under the blankets alone."

His grin shines vibrantly through the phone, "Jacks, you're killing me. I'll page you later. Miss you, baby," and he hangs up. I may have made a date for phone sex, but he'll be paging me from the break room at work.

I finish my workday and meet Dot for coffee. Today coffee means margaritas at her house. I tell her the whole story about my weekend. Every detail from the no-tell motel and waiting for him to get off work to Tiger and initiating sex in my truck without a condom. We spent at least one margarita talking about Tiger. I told her everything. Except, Dot clued in on the problem, "Jackie, are you avoiding the problem on purpose? You seem to honestly like this guy, not just his dick. Are you going to ignore him and not see him again?"

I bow my head down into my hands, "I already agreed to see him again. He asked before I left and I couldn't tell him no. I can't lie to him again. I've already lied too much."

"Don't forget the fact that you want to see him again." Dot's eyes get big and she stares at me, suddenly knowing the truth… "Are you falling?"

"You know falling isn't allowed," I eye her to make my point. She's aware how much I've been dating and what I've been up to the last year.

"I'm glad you got a handle on that, not falling." She laughs at me. "You might want to try looking in the mirror or maybe another drink would do the trick. You look horrified at the position you're in. If you weren't falling, you wouldn't care and you'd keep playing with him if you wanted, until you were done with him." Dot shakes her head at me, she can't believe it.

"What do I do?" I ask her.

"The first question is, what do you want?" She has a point. A plan cannot be formulated without having a defined goal.

Four margaritas, a bag of tortilla chips, and a jar of salsa later, Dot's husband drives me the short distance home in my truck and makes sure I get in safe before he walks home. Overall, he's a good dude. It's early, but I strip naked and go to bed anyway. My brain is drunk and tired.

Hours later my pager goes off at about 2am. At first I'm irritated, then I remember it's Danny and smile as I dial the number to call him back.

"Hello?"

"Hi, baby," I reply in a sleepy British voice.

"Are you in bed?"

"Yes, I'm wrapped in my blanket. But, I'd rather have you wrapped around me."

"I wish I was wrapped around you, too. What are you wearing?" He's talking quietly, and I wonder if there's someone else in the room there.

"Nothing," I say in my sleepy breathless tone. "Danny, are you alone in the break room?"

"No."

"Oh, then you can't say things to me that you want to say?" teasing him.

"That's true."

"I'll have to talk for both of us. I'm guessing you want to hold me right now and kiss me in the way you do that makes me not be able to think."

"More than you know, baby."

I smile, "You probably don't realize how lethal you are for me. It's your kiss, I'm pretty sure it's a mind controlling drug for me."

I hear him fidgeting, "Really?" This strong man showing his insecurity is too sexy.

"Yes, really. I'd never go bare, I blame you for driving me to do mindless things." There's banging on my door, again. What the hell is with the 2am house calls? I ignore it, but it gets louder and the doorbell starts. Son of a bitch!

"I'm hearing a lot of background noise. What's going on over there?"

"Somebody is at the door, they probably have the wrong address or something." Hoping it's enough to make him not ask questions.

"Why don't you check it out while I'm on the phone?"

I don't want to get out of bed. I don't care who's at the door. I don't want to explain Bryan at my door having one of his emotional breakdowns or Rob trying to get me back or either of them after sex or who knows what scenario could lie behind door number three. Mostly, I'm warm and snuggly and have my favorite man on the phone. The rest of them can go to hell. "I'm talking with you right now."

The annoying noise at my door continues, "Please, Jacks. Go check and let me know you're okay."

"Fine." Damn it. I walk to the door and check the peephole to find Bryan with his guitar.

I open the door wrapped in my blanket. "It's after 2am again."

"I know. I'm sorry, Jackie. I've been thinking about what you said and I can't sleep. Can I come in and play a new song for you?"

"No. I'm busy. Call me tomorrow during the hours of normal people and we'll get together."

"Why are you using a British accent again?" Bryan shakes

his head and focuses on me, "Jackie, are you naked wrapped in that blanket?"

"Not for you," and I closed the door.

When I get back to the phone, Danny sounds irritated. "Sorry, I got rid of him."

"There was a guy at your door at 2am?" I can tell he's upset.

"Yes. A friend who plays guitar wanted to play his new song for me."

"I bet that's not all he wanted."

"Doesn't matter. He can want, that doesn't mean he can have."

Danny's tone changes, "Who can have?"

"You, baby. Only you."

Danny sounds irritated, "I want to talk to you more and I want to be there to keep the other guys away, but I'm here and my break is over. I miss you, Jacks. Oh, they've got me scheduled to work this weekend. We'll talk soon." He kisses into the phone when he hangs up.

I fall back asleep without any effort, smiling from ear to ear. Danny misses me.

CHAPTER THIRTEEN

Danny's been scheduled to work off shifts, his own fault because he asked for more hours and I understand, but it makes it hard to connect. It's been quick calls on his break, not being able to talk at the same time, and only one day off at a time, which is not long enough to make the drive to Vegas. He needs time to sleep on his day off and if I'm there, sleep will be forgotten and we could both need a recovery day. Maybe I should take this as a sign to simply let it go and do my best to forget him, my out allowing me to never tell him about my stupid British lie. The world, universe, karma, whatever, is giving me my way out. If only I would take it.

Work has been uneventful, but Bryan is a whole different story. After another 2am visit that got my door slammed in his face and some choice words yelled at him, Bryan got a clue. He actually showed up at my work on Thursday morning with flowers as a peace offering and asked me out to lunch. I swear men are dogs in more ways than one. First, they sniff out any ass they can get. Second, they can tell when another guy is sniffing after you and they want you more. Maybe it's the idea of having a woman in demand. Maybe it's selfishly taking something from someone else, being a bad boy stealing or playing with someone else's toy. Whatever it is, Bryan is focused on the scent and knows what he wants to do with his bone. I agree to lunch because he'll always be a friend. I tell him to pick up food and meet me at my truck at my lunch break.

I walk out to my truck at my lunch break to find Bryan sitting on the hood leaning back against the windshield with his arms crossed behind his head. Normally the sight of Bryan's long, slender body, with wavy dark hair down to his ass, moody green eyes, and sexy artist's hands all stretched out in front of me like a buffet would be all it takes to give him whatever he wants and not even expect anything in return. I admit he looks damn good, but he just isn't doing it for me. He hops down off my truck when I approach and grabs me around the waist, immediately planting a kiss on my lips. This is not our normal patter. This is not how he greets me. This is how a boyfriend should greet his girlfriend, not how friends should greet each other. "Hey baby, I picked up your favorite carnitas tacos."

Hey baby? What the hell is going on here? "Thanks, they smell delicious and I'm hungry. Bryan, what's with the kiss and calling me baby?" I need to nip this in the bud.

"You were mad at me for not treating you right and you're right, you deserve better. So, I'm trying to do better and be what you deserve. I'm not perfect and it'll take time for me to get there. I won't show up at 2am anymore, you're more than a booty call and showing up after midnight is looking for a booty call." He's obviously proud of himself.

How am I going to handle this? I don't want him to leave and I don't want to hurt him. I may want this from him soon. "Bry, we've always been friends and sometimes I've been your booty call. I appreciate your effort, but this is bad timing. We need to stick with being friends and in the not so distant future when my heart is smashed into a zillion pieces, maybe you will help me pick up the pieces?"

"Bad timing? Jackie, you've been on me like flies on shit for years and it's bad timing?" Bryan gives me a crazy stare and grabs my face. "You need to remember how hot the heat is between us." He pulls my face to his and kisses me the way I've always wanted him to kiss me, the way he has buckled my knees in the past and granted him instant access to sex. Not today. He pulls away to get my reaction and his pulse is racing. "Jackie?"

"I'm sorry. It's not like that. If you want to date me, then you should've made an effort before there was another man." Bryan's frustrated by all of this, it's out of his realm. He's used to getting what he wants, and not only from me, but from any female in the crowd at his gigs and any female he plays his guitar for and well, simply put—any female he wants. We lean on my truck together eating tacos and it isn't as comfortable as it usually is between us. I get that he's frustrated, but how does he think I've felt for years? I try to bring him back to friend, "You want to come over tonight and play your new song for me?"

"I have practice tonight and gigs this weekend, it'll be too late tonight." Imagine that, he learns!

I talk to Danny a few times over the weekend, including a couple times when he isn't at work. One time when I called him back he told me Tony wasn't home and asked me what I was wearing, I talked dirty to him for almost an hour and we had phone sex. Another time, I suggested I might be too much trouble for him and he should forget about me. It made him mad, even though I pointed out he's hot and could probably have any woman he wanted. He told me he found the woman he wanted and his work schedule wasn't going to keep him from having her.

The problem is his work schedule has him working five or six days per week, including weekends for the next few weeks. It had been almost a month since we'd been together, when I called him and he said he had off from 6pm on Friday until noon on Sunday. I was getting used to the phone relationship and had even stopped worrying about my lie—I wasn't going to be with him again. Don't get me wrong, I want to be with him, I miss him, I want him and I'd be lying if I said I didn't cry myself to sleep some nights when the reality of it all hits me at once. I'm hiding from my reality because it hurts too much and I want him, regardless of what I've tried to convince myself. It's easier to pretend the problem, my lie, doesn't matter anymore. I still have him on the phone. Sometimes our long talks make us closer, we get to know each other more intimately and be there for each other for trivial daily stuff. We're comfortable with each other.

Bryan has become persistent, but I haven't given in. I've been to some of his gigs. He's been over to play guitar and have me sing with him. He's brought lunch to me at work at least once a week. He hasn't shown up at unacceptable times. He did kiss me again and offered to give me a massage because I "seemed tense." I allowed the massage and made sure he kept his hands to appropriate parts, but not the sex he wanted to follow it.

Bryan makes me think about Danny. Is Danny hanging out with other women? Having sex and giving "massages"? Bringing girls lunch or flowers to their work? Having women over to spend the night with him and hang out in his cocoon of a fort under the blankets in his bed? Making them shake with pleasure and scream out his name? Letting another girl touch him and lick his tattoo? Kissing someone senseless that isn't me? Taking somebody else to have special pancakes? Damn it! I miss him and I don't want to share him! Am I leading Bryan on? Is what I'm doing fair to either one of them, or even me?

We all know the truth, well I know the truth and you know the truth, but the guys don't. I should forget about Danny because he's into the idea of having a British girl. Bryan wants me the way I am and he's right here, easily accessible, and making a noticeable effort to be what I deserve. They (whoever they are) always say relationships that start with friendship are the best relationships. By that definition, I'd say Bryan is the better choice, except we've been friends with benefits since the day we met and I was sure that nobody would make me want them the way he does—until I met Danny. He completely erased my Bryan memories and I mean he demolished the memories into no longer decipherable atomic particles.

CHAPTER FOURTEEN

The week goes quickly and I'm happy, almost to the point of giddy while I count down the minutes until I will be with Danny. I put in a request at work to get off work early on Friday and offer to work extra hours the other days to make up for it.

Bryan came by my place on Tuesday evening to play guitar, which I always enjoy. It's perfect for both of us because he doesn't have band practice on Tuesday night and I love to sing. Someday my singing will be more than choir and my living room. He greeted me with a hug and blinked at me, "I'm happy to see you smiling. You haven't smiled in weeks." I could almost see it click in his brain. "You haven't smiled since you started telling me no." Okay, maybe he didn't quite get it. "I can put a smile on your face, baby. Let me take you on a real date this weekend and give me a chance. What do you say?"

How do I do this? IImmm… "It sounds nice, but I'm going out of town this weekend." I like it, nondescript.

"Well, then let me put a smile on your face right now," Bryan puts his arms around my neck and kisses my cheek tenderly. "I promise it'll be different. I want you, Jackie," he whispers in my ear.

Where the hell was this a year ago or even three months ago, when there was nothing I wanted more? Oh, that's right— Bryan was busy sticking it into as many girls as he could.

"I don't think it's the best idea. I'm afraid you want me because I won't let you have me and I'm not interested." I focus on Bryan imploring him to understand what I'm saying.

Bryan follows me into my bedroom, talking to me while I finish a load of laundry, when he stops in his tracks. He scans my room, seeing the Ramone's T-shirt I've been wearing every night laying on my pillow, and my pager blinking on my night-stand. He picks up my pager, "Whose pager is this? Someone wants a call back to Las Vegas." His wheels are turning and he's not happy. At one time, I stole his T-shirts. "Jackie, does the owner of the Ramone's shirt live in Vegas?"

"It's my shirt and I live here." Obstinate, difficult, and putting off the inevitable, defines me.

"That shirt is at least two sizes too big for you and we both know you steal shirts from guys when you're into them. I never did get my Nirvana shirt back." He's frustrated, but it's divided by sad and pissed.

"I may have imported it from Vegas."

"Tell me you're not going to Vegas this weekend." His emotional side is showing and it's a strange experience. I've never been the cause, I've only been the cure.

"I can't tell you that."

"Damn it, Jackie! I'm trying here. I'm trying to be right for you and you're seeing another guy."

My frustration sets in, "Look, I told you there was another guy and I told you I doubt it'll last long and I told you I hope you're there to pick up my pieces. When this is over, I'm going to be broken and I'm going to need you. But, I'm not walking away from him until I have to. And, Bryan, I'll have to walk away from him because I did something that's for sure a deal breaker and when I confess, he'll never want to see me, talk to me, or even remember my existence. So, if you want to know why I haven't been smiling—I fell for a guy I lied to and now I'm fucked!" Did I just say I fell for a guy? I don't fall. There must be some miscommunication or maybe I'm exaggerating for Bryan's benefit. That must be it, impact for Bryan. "I think about it almost every day. The reason I'm smiling this week is because I'm going to visit him. It's the first time in a month we have a day off at the same time and I'm even getting off work early to go. I know this sounds stupid and I'm more sensible than this, but that's how bad this is. Just walk away or whatever it is you're going to do."

Bryan tosses my pager onto my bed and glares at me with hurt in his eyes.

"I'm sorry. I've never lied to you and I never will. I'd rather you leave and never talk to me again having been honest. But, I hope you understand and remember I told you there was another guy. I hope you're patient with me." It's the truth. If nothing else, I've learned you can't lie. Lies require too much effort and too much maintenance. Friendships cannot be built on lies. Sometimes little things seem fun and insignificant, but end up being more than they seem.

Bryan left my room and sat on my couch playing his guitar for a few minutes before he stood up and left. Not sure what I expected, but I'm not surprised at his actions.

CHAPTER FIFTEEN

On Thursday, I talk with Danny and tell him I'll be leaving at lunch on Friday, so I can pick him up from work. "I'm anxious to see you, Jacks. I know this sounds bad, but I want my hands on your body. I want to hold you close. I miss you, baby. I got us our own room at Excalibur, it'll be just us and there will be no working around Tony. I prepaid and added your name to the room, so if you get here early you can pick up a key." He misses me and I miss him, too. We want the same things. It makes me happy.

"It sounds perfect, Danny. Except, I want to do more—I want to kiss you. I want to lick you. I want you hard and in me. Does that work for you?"

Danny's voice is raspy, "Yes. Fuck. Yes. You just made me hard."

"Then we're even because I'm wet." I say to him playfully.

"Jacks, you're killing me. Remember to pick me up in front tomorrow, away from the creeps."

"Awe, I was looking forward to the creeps. You walking out the side door straight to me, taking me in your arms and kissing me stupid while you lift me off of the ground, bringing my mouth level with yours and wrapping my legs around you. Imagine their reactions, especially when they hear me moan at your touch."

"Fine. Pick me up at the side door, but stay in your truck with the door locked until you see me come out, okay?"

"Yes, sir."

"You drive me crazy, baby. You have no idea how much I miss you. It's been too long, and it can't happen again. I wish you were closer."

"Someday."

Thursday night I go through my bag to make sure I have everything I need and plan to dress up sexy for him when I pick him up from work. I mean, why not? Right? I have to stay in my truck until he's there anyway. I rummage through my closet for something to catch my eye. I'm thinking skirt and it hits me he's a metal head, change up a Hollywood dive outfit. I find my shortest denim mini skirt, it's slightly tattered around the bottom edge, buttons up the front, and fits snug enough around my ass to make it look good while still being almost too short. My black deep scoop tank is clingy and will be great with it. I'll take my denim jacket just in case, but bare arms and maybe flip-flops would be perfect. I'll be sexy and relaxed. I need to pack a snack bag, because I doubt we leave the room.

Friday is a blur and I'm pulling out of the parking lot at noon. I already have everything in my truck and a full tank of gas. I hit the freeway quick and munch on my brown-bagged lunch during my drive. I have more packed and with me this time than I did last time. I probably won't need any of it, but it's Vegas and I want to be prepared for whatever Danny might have planned. I love the drive to Vegas when the rest of the traffic hasn't joined me yet. I've got my new "Best of Foreigner" CD playing for my drive. I'm happy. I feel free. I can't wait to get to Danny.

I make the whole drive without stopping and find parking at Excalibur a few minutes after 4pm. I toss my bags over my shoulder and walk through the casino to the front desk. The front desk is busy, but doesn't take too long to get to me. I ask them if they have a key waiting for me and give them my name. They hand me an envelope and tell me to enjoy my stay. I walk away and open the envelope to find a room key with a sticky note stuck to it with room number 1121 written on it. I take the elevator up to unlock the room and get settled. The message light on the phone is blinking, so I retrieve the message to find Danny saying "See you at 6pm, Jacks. Side door and please stay in your truck. Can't wait to see you."

I unpack and change into my sexy skirt for Danny. I brush out my hair and give it a twirl with my curling iron. Since I have time, I go ahead and put on my make-up, too. I go heavy on the eyeliner, I'm in Vegas after all. I'm happy with my outfit and it's warm out, so I go with flip-flops and no jacket. I take off for the side door at the Stardust and double-park, Danny can't miss me right when he steps out of the building. I stay in my truck like a good girl, and have the hard rock station playing loud. It's 5:55pm and a few workers have already started to leave the building. I roll my window down and watch for Danny. When I start to wonder if the same creepy guy will be here or different creeps or if this will be a creep-free encounter, a guy who resembles the same creep walks out the door and hangs out smoking. A few minutes later, my hot Danny comes walking out with a bag over his shoulder and already changed into street clothes.

I need to elaborate. It seems Danny had the same idea I had and wanted to look hot for me. He's wearing his perfect fitting

Levi's 501 jeans, a snug black T-shirt, sunglasses similar to Ray-Ban Wayfarers, and he's been letting his hair grow out. Freaking hot!

I jump out of my truck and walk a few steps toward him, pretty much ready to jump his bones right there in the parking lot during broad daylight. His face lights up as soon as he sees me and there's an immediate reaction in his pants. I couldn't have asked for more. I guess Tiger missed me, too.

As soon as Danny is within my reach I have my hands on him and his hands are on me. I reach my hands around his neck and he puts his arms around my waist, lifting me to his needy lips. I wrap my legs around him and kiss him back greedily, sliding my tongue into his mouth and grinding my sex against his bulge. It all drives me to a whimper right there in the parking lot, and I find myself calling out his name, "Oh, Danny... I've missed you."

The creep by the door starts in, "Again, what do you want with this guy? You should try me."

"No, thank you," I yell out. "Only Danny, and I need to go get him out of these jeans now. Have a good evening." Danny still holds me with my legs wrapped around him.

Danny whispers in my ear, "Have I told you how fucking amazing you are? You make me indestructible." I smile at the power I have.

"Do you have plans for us this weekend?" I'm wondering if there's anything I need to be prepared for.

"Yeah, mostly naked plans," he chuckles. "I thought you might want to go dancing later tonight or tomorrow night. I just want to be with you, baby. It's fun dancing with you." He's smiling and holding me, not wanting to let me go.

"Let's get out of here," I suggest. He puts me down and we both get in my truck. His hand is on my thigh for the ride to

Excalibur, he slides it under the short hem of my skirt to graze my wet heat.

"Fuck, you're so wet." He slides a finger along the edge of my panties and I spread my legs for him while I'm driving. He slides his finger under the lace of my panties and along my wet heat. He shivers and I watch him put the finger in his mouth to lick it clean. Fucking killing me! Are we there yet? He slides his finger under the lace again, but this time he slides it right into me and repeats the pulling it out and licking it clean process. "You taste so good, and all I want to do is be in you," he says while he slides two fingers in me and strokes into me repeatedly, occasionally spreading his fingers apart. Driving to Excalibur I run a red light and slam the brakes twice. "That's it, Jacks. I want you ready for me when we get there. I need to be in you." Danny pulls his fingers out when I park my truck and sucks them clean. We walk into the hotel with his arm around me, holding me at his side, and straight to the elevator. He hits the button for the 11th floor and everyone else exits on the 4th. Danny pulls the elevator stop and drops to his knees, enjoying the easy access of my extreme mini skirt. He pulls my panties to the side and puts his mouth on me, sucking everywhere he can reach. He slides his two fingers back in me and I tremble. He licks my sensitive nub, once, twice, then sucks on it hard while he strokes me with his fingers and I completely lose it. He has to hold me up to keep me from falling and I'm screaming out his name. He stops, stands, and takes my mouth with his, to muffle my cries and backs me to the corner of the elevator as he reaches back and gets the elevator moving again. Pinned between Danny and the wall is an amazing place to be, his hard muscles are against me and he's the only thing keeping me standing. We get to the 11th floor. Danny holds his arm around me while we walk to our room and unlock the door. It's a new experience for us to have the privacy of our own room and it's different because we've had a month to get to know each other. I need to tell him I'm not British, but I'm not going to. I don't want to lose him and I've exceeded all rational time limits for confessing. Before the door can lock behind us, Danny has his hands all over me, grasping for purchase and kissing me greedily. His heart is racing and his pulse pounding. He drops his bag on the dresser, unzips it and makes the box of condoms accessible. Grabbing one and tossing it on the bed, he stops and focuses on me sitting at the foot of the bed. I reach toward him and he walks to me. I bite his button fly with my teeth and pull his jeans open, one button at a time. I push his jeans down enough to give Tiger some room and kiss him on the tip, taking his tip in my mouth and swirling around him with my tongue. I trace his hard shaft lightly with my fingers, remembering how thick and hard he is. He watches me closely, with his eyes focused on my mouth.

"I know what you want right now," I say to him, "you should get what you want." He's watching me. I turn around and start to crawl up to the pillow, but instead I stay on all fours, back up to the edge of the bed and hike my skirt up a couple of inches. "Danny, will you pull my panties off please?"

"Fuck me," He says as he puts his hand on my ass, squeezing both cheeks and rubbing his hard length against my wetness. He hooks his fingers in my panties at each of my hips and pulls them off, dropping them to the floor. "Jacks, I don't think you're ready for me like this."

"Do you want something different, Danny?"

"This is exactly what I want, but I'll hurt you if I take you the way I want to right now. I never want to hurt you, baby."

"Just do it. Please, Danny. Please fuck me. Fuck me hard. I want you pounding against me so hard I can't hold myself up. I know you want to make me scream, make me call your name so loud they can hear me on the 8th floor." His eyes go dark with glowing flames as he slides into me, but he's right and he can't get inside me all the way. I rub back against him pushing him to go further with each stroke and I feel him stretching me—he's amazing.

"I missed you around me. It's stupid because we only had the weekend, but the only sex I want is you. You're so tight. You're made to work perfectly for me." He holds a tight grip on my hips and slams into me until he can get the rest of the way in, needing to be buried inside me.

I scream out, "Yes, Danny! Fuck me more."

He curses under his breath and leans over me, biting my shoulder from behind while he strokes into me. I spread my knees allowing him deeper access and reach between my legs to stroke him as he enters me. His breath is ragged, "I've missed you, baby. I've missed us."

"Jacks, touch yourself and make yourself come hard around me while I'm fucking you. Do it, I need you." I move my hand and find how stretched I am to accommodate his huge cock and what it's doing to my clit. I'm luxuriously full and beyond happy to be back in Danny's arms with him buried deep inside me. I touch myself lightly, so sensitive I can hardly stand it. Then I rub harder in time with his strokes and stop when I get close. I start again, rubbing it harder and faster, uncontrollably until I'm crying out and my body is clenching at Danny so hard he's moaning and calling out my name. His arm around my waist is the only thing holding me up as he catches me before I collapse to the bed. "Oh, Jacks—you're fucking amazing," barely able to speak while he pounds into me a few last times and rides out his orgasm. We collapse in a heap on the bed, limbs entangled, both of us breathing hard and trying to recover.

CHAPTER SIXTEEN

I was hoping it wouldn't be like this. I was hoping the weekend we spent together was a fluke with the extra excitement of being new and unknown. I was hoping he'd be different than I remembered, different than I've built him up to be over the last month. We always make people better than they are in our mind compared to reality. Danny is everything I remember and more. He's better than what I made him to be in my mind. His only flaw is location, or maybe it's my flaw. The only thing that matters is this thing we have between us, and I can't explain it, somehow we belong together.

Danny rolls toward me and tucks my hair behind my ear, "Do you want to go out with me tonight? Let me take you out for some fun. Dinner, dancing, drinking, people watching, anything you want."

"Are you sure you want me to put clothes on?" I ask him teasingly.

"I wanted to take you out before and when we went out it was because we had to get out during the day. I want to go out tonight with you on my arm, as a couple. We don't have to stay out all night. We can see where the night takes us and we always have tomorrow to stay in bed."

"Sounds fun. Let's go dancing." I smile at him and I'm getting kind of excited, but I'm not sure if it's the going out or simply being with him. "How long do I have to get ready? Do I have a dress code?"

"This is Las Vegas, you can wear whatever you want. I'm going to shower, and should be ready in about half an hour. You take as long as you need, baby."

I'm glad I packed too much, it'll be fun to get dressed up to go out dancing with Danny in Vegas. One, I'm with Danny and won't have to worry about guys harassing me. Two, what will make Danny crazy all night while we are out? I already wore my denim mini skirt. I shuffle through what I brought, fluff out my hair and change my make-up while Danny is in the shower. I put on my matching black satin bra and panties. I pull on my thigh-high black suede boots, my favorite for dancing.

Danny walks out of the bathroom, "Fuck you're hot." I get happy all over and keep getting ready. He looks like sin itself dressed in his dark jeans and black button up shirt. I know he's watching me as I pull my fitted black dress from the closet, slide it over my head and shimmy it into place. The bottom edge skims my thigh about six inches above my boots. The dress laces up at my breasts, but it fits a bit tight there and I leave the laces loose, revealing.

I turn to him sweetly, "Can you zip me up please?"

Danny walks toward me and runs his hands over my body, appreciating my curves and the soft material of my dress. Staring at me with heat in his hooded eyes, he takes in every inch of me, possibly reconsidering his plan to go out. He leans in and kisses my neck. He finds his way to my back and the zipper, admiring the bare skin from my neck down to the curve of my ass where the zipper starts. He puts his hands on my bare shoulders and runs them down my back to the zipper, finally zipping me up tight. I glance in the mirror, then at Danny and I've succeeded on my mission. "You take my breath away, Jacks. How did I ever manage to deserve you?" He stands next to me when I take in our reflection in the mirror and the picture of us together staggers me. Both dressed in black, red cheeked, his hands on me adoringly, his lips on my neck, me leaning into him, desire between us. This is what a couple looks like, connected.

Danny takes my arm affectionately and leads me to the casino. We stop at the bar and he gets us each a Midori and Sprite. He checks the time and takes my hand leading me out into the Las Vegas night. We cross over the strip to the Tropicana, then cross Tropicana Avenue to the MGM and enter the casino. I realize where we're going when we walk up to a crowd. He's taking us back to the lounge where we met and the same crazy lounge entertainer who got us both on the dance floor is playing tonight. That guy was obnoxious, but he did play some awesome music and, well, I'm not complaining because he brought me Danny. The act was going to start soon, you could already hear the music playing and there's a line waiting to get in. Danny walks up to the entrance, high-fives the guy at the door and we're the first two in. He chooses a table at the front, on the edge of the dance floor. He places the two chairs next to each other and puts his arm around me when we sit down. It's loud when the waitress comes over. He orders drinks and she marks the table reserved for us. He sits there staring at me in a haze, with a shit-eating grin, his hand caressing my waist. We watch the place fill up and the waitress brings us our drinks. The Vegas crowd is always entertaining, different levels of dress and intoxication. We enjoy laughing together, but the mood changes when Danny gazes into my eyes. Trying to read his mind when he leans in and presses his lips to mine. It's a cross between "what was I thinking going out tonight" and "what are we doing, Jacks?" and the realization, "I'm falling". He sucks down about half his drink quickly and claims my mouth with his, he can't get enough of me. The obnoxious guy with the bad hair starts his routine.

"Hey blondie! Get up and dance with her before you suck her face. You can suck face later. My show is only a couple hours long." Danny holds his hand out to me and we are on the dance floor enjoying the groove of Wild Cherry's "Play That Funky Music". "Blondie, I think I remember you two. Did I make a love connection? Isn't she one of my Dazzey Duks girls?" Danny nods and gives Mr. Obnoxious a thumbs up. "It's amazing the work I do here, best music anywhere and now I'm a matchmaker." He turns to his band and yells, "Johnny, remind me to have 'Matchmaker' added to my business cards and resume." I laugh while we dance and turn my ass to Danny, rubbing against him to the beat. He puts his hands on my hips and moves with me. "This next one is for the two kissy faces, I understand if you can't help yourselves when you hear my smooth tones."

"Waiting For a Girl Like You" by Foreigner comes through the speakers and it makes me smile, remembering Danny singing it to me late in the night while he held me in his bed. Danny pulls me close and we sway together. He kisses me tenderly until the lyrics start, then he sings in my ear and his hot breath sends shivers down my spine. This time he sings all the words. I try not to get into my head, but I'd be lying if I said it didn't make me a sappy gooey girl when he sang the lines he left out before. I can be such a girl.

We dance together for the first set, having a fun time.

Laughing together. Touching each other. Kissing. Our bodies in sync. Watching each other. At the end of the first set we sit at our table and finish our drinks. Danny orders another round and shots of whiskey. The waitress is back quickly with the drinks. Danny wasn't kidding when he said drinking tonight. He challenges me, "I'm betting you can shoot whiskey. If not, we can share with Mr. Obnoxious."

Does he think I can't shoot whiskey? Is he trying to get me going and pick on me or what? "I can do more shots than you." I glare at him with a challenge in my eyes and wonder why I get myself into these things. Someday I'll learn to ignore a challenge, but it obviously isn't going to be tonight.

Danny laughs, "We're on drink three and no food, so let's stick with two shots each and see what happens. Ready? One, two, three!" we clink the glasses and do a shot each. "Okay, next one. One, two, three!" clink and down goes the second shot.

The alcohol hits me when I take a big drink of my third Midori and Sprite. I don't care. It's nice to be loose, free, uninhibited. I stand up and straddle Danny's lap, leaning over to kiss his lips. Both of us taste of melon and whiskey. His hands are on my hips while I control the kiss, passionately sucking on his tongue and lips. He urges me down to his lap and I sit with his cock hard beneath me. My legs are on either side of him and my front is plastered to his, we're both breathing hard with desire. I want him badly, and I wonder if that's the point of going out—the build up of having to wait because you can't have sex in public. Well, you aren't supposed to have sex in public, but it's a real possibility. It wouldn't be the first time. When you think about it, dancing makes it worse since it's basically sex standing up with your clothes on. I sit on his lap and we make out until the music starts back up. The place is a mad house and so full nobody even notices how hot and heavy we are.

"Ladies and gentlemen, it's time for the second hour of the best show on the strip—but, you're here and stuck with me! So get your asses out on the dance floor and shake it!" Mr. Obnoxious starts singing a medley of Rod Stewart tunes, funny because his hair is reminiscent of the same Woody Woodpecker hair design.

Danny stands, picking me up and carrying me with him to the dance floor. We're in a haze together, and in my current state I can't tell you if it's the alcohol or simply desire. We dance together and are in control, until they play a few slow songs in a row, "Here's a few to get you lovers out there in the mood. You can thank me later, guys. Ladies, just call out my name later. A couple of you don't need the help. You know who you are." The band plays "Always and Forever" by Heat Wave, followed by "Into the Night" by Benny Mardones, then "Endless Love" by Diana Ross and Luther Vandross. Switching up the set with "Holding on to Yesterday" by Ambrosia, and I love how the band has changed it up, giving it more of a rock edge and a dirty groove. Danny and I don't need the encouragement, it fuels our fire and we can't keep our hands off one another. We hold on tight, even when the music gets faster we're melded together. A pry bar couldn't get between us. The dancing becomes dirty, grinding against each other, his leg between mine, his hand on my ass and mine feeling his abs through his shirt. The heat is undeniable, and the need out of control. It reminds me of high school when you'd been making out with your long time boyfriend and finally did it for the first time, you had to, you needed to be together and the unknown was exciting and scary at the same time. There was no stopping then and there would be no stopping all night long tonight. Danny pulls my body to his tightly, wrapping both of his arms around me. Claiming me as his own with his actions and taking my mouth with his. He lifts my leg and wraps it around him, holding me up while we dance. His mouth continues to devour mine, then moves to my neck. The sheer pleasure of it causes me to throw my head back, allowing access to my neck and cleavage. He moves his kiss to my cleavage, enjoying the top of my soft round breasts as they gently bounce.

"Geez! You two are making me hot and bothered. Get a room already." Danny takes Mr. Obnoxious's suggestion, taking my hand and leading me out of the lounge.

Walking through the casino, Danny stops suddenly in the middle of everything and turns me to face him, as if we are in our own world and a continuous line of people doesn't have to walk around us. He holds both of my hands and stares into my eyes, with words on the tip of his tongue and nothing coming out. Searching for answers or direction. I stretch up to kiss him gently on the lips, "Can we go home, Danny?" His expression changes, he got the answer he needed and it's what he wanted—me.

CHAPTER SEVENTEEN

On the way back to our room, we stop on the pedestrian bridge to take in the view of the Las Vegas Strip. The lights, the crowd, the noise, the buildings, and the landmarks that make this Las Vegas. There's something romantic about it, even though there are thousands of people, some of which are handing out flyers for escorts, many of them drunk, and it kind of smells. I guess it's the love all around you. All of the chapels. All of the couples getting married. The bachelors and bachelorettes, out partying as single people for the last time. The brides in their formal gowns rushing to limousines with their bridesmaids who are dressed in less fortunate gowns. The grooms hanging out at the bar near the casino chapel in their tux and sometimes tennis shoes, waiting for their future wife to get there. Marriage is a twenty-four hours per day, seven days per week business here. The beautiful flowers, the cakes, and the loud wedding parties in the restaurants. Las Vegas runs on love, there isn't a bigger gamble. Matchmaker might be the perfect skill to have here.

We stand on the bridge facing North up the strip, Danny's behind me and has his arms around me with his head resting on my shoulder. The cool, outdoor air has cleared our heads, allowing us some self-control. He kisses my neck and turns me to him, taking me in his arms and kissing me senseless. I push my breasts against his chest and vine my leg around his, grazing his hard length. Tiger is obviously hanging to the right and I move my hand along his jeans lightly stroking. Danny lets out a low moan and pulls me closer. I want more, I need him. I unbutton his jeans and slide my hand down to Tiger, grasping him and stroking him with my fingers. I whisper to Danny, "Do you want my hands on you like this? Do you like me stroking your huge cock in public? I bet you'd like it if I dropped to my knees and sucked you off right here. Or, maybe you'd prefer to take me in my short sexy dress and push into me discreetly, unbutton your jeans and wrap me around your waist and your cock." His already hooded eyes get darker.

He kisses me hard on the lips, then moves to my neck, kissing, biting, sucking. His tone heavy and sexy in my ear, "I want to do all of it, but not here. I want you to myself. I don't want to share you. I want all the way inside you. I want to make you scream out my name. I want you to know I'm the only one for you. I want you to need me. I'm going to make you beg me for more. I know you want me to touch you. I know you want me to lick you. You want me to take your breast in my mouth and suck hard. You want me to bury my face in your wet heat and drive you to ecstasy with my tongue. But, you're a girl and what you want most," his tone changes, softer and filled with—something else, "you want to feel how much I care about you. You want to know in your heart this is more than sex. You want to be loved. I want to give you everything, Jacks." I kiss him, trying to show him what he means to me without words and his lips smile against mine. I wrap my arms around his neck as he lifts me and carries me to our room.

We get in the elevator and he kisses me, stroking my tongue with his while he holds me tight. We get to our floor and the door opens. He sets me down and holds me up against the hallway wall with desire. Rubbing his body against mine, needy, teasing my breasts, my heat on his thigh. Pressing his lips to mine with sex, desire, need, heat, all of it rolling off of him. My body screams for joy internally in anticipation of what will come next. His breathing on the ragged edge, he stops himself and hurries to our room. I walk into our room in front of him and bend over, glancing back at him from down between my legs. He moans audibly. He reaches for me and he slides a finger under the hem of my panties, sliding it into me while he releases Tiger with the other. He slides my dress up and pulls my panties down. He's ready to take me, but he surprises me by dropping to his knees and putting his mouth on me. Licking and sucking at my clit and my wet folds. Burying his face in my wetness and digging in with his tongue. Making low noises and causing vibrations to run through me. "Please, Danny. Please. I want you." It doesn't take anymore than that, but his attitude changes. He stands up and turns me to him, kissing me tenderly, showing me he wants me. He leads me to the bed and pulls my boots off, then my panties. He unzips my dress and pulls it off of me. He unhooks my bra and sends it flying across the room. He kicks his shoes off and pushes his pants down, stepping out of them. Always commando, he starts unbuttoning his shirt and it may be the sexiest thing I've ever seen. I gesture for him to come to me and I slowly work the buttons on his shirt blindly while we kiss. Our kiss is hot and full of desire. I move to his sexy chest and kiss him there, licking his chest all over and getting him to lie down on the bed. Kissing his nipples and his tattoo before I lick my way to his happy trail. I kiss him with wet open-mouthed kisses along his trail and take care, trying to go slow. Tiger is getting harder and bending toward me. I lick the end of his cock teasingly and he grabs me, lifting my hips and placing my sex on his mouth. His tongue is amazing and motivates me to move on Tiger. I take him in my mouth as deep as I can, which doesn't even get me half way down his shaft, and I suck on him hard, stroking him with my tongue. I lick him from end to end repeatedly and suck on his tip, bobbing on him and stroking him with my lips. He licks my sensitive nub and starts to suck, driving my intensity. "Oh, Danny. Please. Please more. Don't you want to be inside me?" He groans and he sucks at me harder and harder, swiping his tongue back and forth across me. I try to pull away, so I can slide onto his hard dick, but he's holding me in place and won't let me move. I scream out at the realization, but it only pushes him further. Licking and sucking hard, while he holds me to his mouth even tighter. "Oh, baby. That's right, you're in control. Take me, Danny. Take me." His hands move up and down my body. He rolls me off of him and pulls me to him, I climb on top of him and straddle him, sliding onto his hard cock slowly and completely. Grinding against him, moaning with each delicious stroke. I'm so sensitive and I can hardly stand it, feeling absolutely everything. He's huge inside me, stretching me and hitting my sweet spot, and he'd be bigger if he was taking me. "Oh Danny! How can you be so big and hard?" Whimpering with every movement.

"Stay with me, Jacks. You're unbelievable around me. I swear I get harder for you. Keep moving, baby. You're perfect around me and this hard, I feel everything." He takes my hips, guiding me to what he wants. He's amazing and somehow knows what I want, making me want more.

"You're so… Oh, Danny."

"It's okay, baby. Don't hold back. I've got you. All night long, baby. I promise. It doesn't have to stop. Over and over, I'll make you happy." Danny's breathing heavy. "Do you feel how deep inside you I am? Feel how thick I am rubbing inside you. That's how happy you make me. Come for me now, baby, and I'll follow you over the edge. You're my girl, Jacks. I need you. You make me think about things I've never wanted before. You bring me to a new level of happy." He pushes into me hard a few times and it's all it takes to have me calling out his name. He keeps going faster and I fall over the edge with his name on my lips, grasping at him, needing him, desiring his kiss. "Yeah, Jacks. Oh, Jacks you're perfect. Fuck me." He searches for my lips needing my kiss as much as I need his.

When we come up for air, Danny laughs at me, "I need to buy you dinner."

"Seriously? Guilty? You owe me or something?" Faking a nasty glare at him, "Kind of the cart before the horse, don't you think?"

Still laughing, "I've been listening to your stomach growl for awhile now. Are you hungry, babe?"

I've been betrayed by my own body in yet another way. "Yes."

"Okay, you pick: casino coffee shop, room service, or we can try to order pizza."

"Hmmm, is it too late for Keno? It doesn't matter. Coffee shop."

Danny gazes at me for a few minutes before taking action. "You know the problem with this plan?"

"I believe I do. It means we have to get out of bed. I don't want to get out of bed."

"Worse, it means we have to get dressed and I want you naked." Danny's tone almost has me choosing sex instead of food.

"I have a plan. I'll suffer the pain of getting out of bed and get dressed so you won't have much to take off of me when we get back. I mean, definitely no panties. What do you say? I do love coffee shop food."

Danny eyes me curious, "You get out of bed and get dressed. I want to see it before I agree." His dirty grin tells me he wants to watch me wander the room naked. I'm willing to oblige and it'll make it harder on him. I get out of bed pulling the sheet with me, playing with him and trying to cover myself, but he isn't having any of it. Danny holds the sheet and I yell out when he pulls it away from me. Teasing him, I bend over in front of him and spread my feet wide, while I pretend I'm getting something from the bottom of the closet. Making small talk with him to make sure he watches me. I get my cut-off sweats, and pull them on adding a cuff to the hem, making them short shorts. I find my bra and put it on. I search for the perfect shirt and realize he was wearing it. I find the black button up he was wearing and put it on, leaving it unbuttoned a button too far on purpose, tucking and tying the bottom to make it fitted at my waist and turning up the sleeves. The shirt is big on me, but I'm not interested in impressing anyone other than Danny and this will show everyone I'm his.

"What do you say, Danny? Only three pieces of clothing, one of them is yours, and I'm still mostly bare for you." I turn to him, "Too trashy?"

"You look good in my shirt, but I'm not sure about those

shorts. You should come over here." Danny moves to the edge of the bed and sits with his feet on the floor.

I walk over to him and do a turn, trying to get a view in the mirror and to see what's wrong with them. "What's wrong with them?" I ask not finding the problem.

"Turn around and I'll fix it," Danny says and I follow orders like a good soldier. Danny puts both of his hands on my ass, "These shorts are soft and very short. Let me see here…" he slides his hands up my shorts directly to my heat. "Umm, they might be fine. I need to check one more thing. Can you bend over please?" I try to keep a straight face and not chuckle when I bend over in front of him.

"What do you think? Will this work?" I ask playing along with him. Enjoying his hands on me, I expect him to slide a finger inside me, but he slides his hard cock right up my shorts and into me.

"Oh yeah, Jacks. This will work just fine." He grabs me by the hips and bounces me against him. Sliding his cock in and out, faster and faster. Not holding anything back. Standing still and using my body for his pleasure. Each pass drives me crazy. Each stroke hits my sweet spot. His fingers dig into my hips harder and harder, his fingernails in his grip. He's breathing hard and I'm already seeing the explosions in my closed eyes. There's an animal element to it, pushing us closer and making us need each other, need to touch, need to connect, need our personal intimate connection. "Jacks. Jacks. Ohhh!"

"I got us, Danny." But, there's no response. I glance back at him and his expression tells me he isn't with me at the moment. I move on him, stroking him inside me slowly. "You're the best, Danny."

After a few minutes he rejoins the party, "Jacks, you do crazy things to me. All of a sudden, I have to have you. It's all I can do and nothing else matters." My stomach growls at him. "Fuck! Sorry, let's go get food."

"Don't be sorry. You make me crazy and I don't even remember I'm hungry."

Danny quickly pulls on his jeans and a T-shirt. I straighten my shorts, deciding they'll still be okay for the coffee shop.

CHAPTER EIGHTEEN

We head to the coffee shop before we get distracted. Eleven floors in the elevator takes forever, Danny tastes my lips softly. "I want to please you. Make you feel good all over," he talks to me quietly and sincerely in his sex voice.

Danny takes my hand when the elevator opens and we walk across the casino to the coffee shop. The smell of food makes my stomach growl when the waitress seats us. There's nothing like a late night coffee shop menu, limited and offering everything you want to eat even though you shouldn't. Danny orders their late night steak and eggs special, and a chocolate milkshake. I order chili cheese fries and a Dr. Pepper, with a plan to steal his shake.

We sit in the booth with our fingers intertwined and at the moment when I'm happier than I've ever been, my head gets in the way—reminding me why I'm not happy, I would be happy if I was British and working in the studios. My head is telling the truth, but I—aw, fuck it! Who am I kidding? I don't want to tell Danny. I love the adventure and freedom of being something or someone I'm not. I don't want to hurt Danny and it's wrong, but nothing lasts forever. It's a cycle. Meet a guy. Maybe get to be friends with a guy. Fuck the guy. Possibly get a repeat fuck. Maybe date for a few months. There might be an illusion of some type of relationship. He might refer to you as his girl or even his girlfriend. Could meet his friends. Only meet his family if he needs a date to a wedding or something. Meet a new guy and repeat. Or, get dumped and mope for a week before you go fuck every guy you know in a week's time and eat gallons of ice cream for dinner to get over it. I don't fall. They're men. There's always another one. None of them are irreplaceable. There's always at least one in line waiting for my attention. He's a man. Half the people in the world are men. Nothing more than another cock to fuck me and another mouth to kiss me. Some are better than others, but there's always another one out there who can match them.

Danny stares at me funny, he's kind of hazy. He draws a line down my nose with his finger and runs his thumb across my lips. "You're so beautiful." He holds my face and kisses me tenderly, sweetly and slowly moving from one edge of my mouth to the other, making sure I taste the same all over and I'm not hiding a secret sweet spot.

Who am I kidding? I'm fucked. Danny is the exception, or maybe he's my exception. I don't believe in the "one" and if I did then I fucked my chance at happiness with a British fucking accent! I've been head over heels for Bryan and he wants me now that I have Danny, but I'm not interested and his kiss doesn't even do it for me anymore. Yep. Fucked. Damn it. Damn it. Damn it. I may need some rum for my Dr. Pepper. Or, maybe I can put a hit out on the part of my brain that likes to remind me about what I've done and forget about it. That's it. Go back to ignoring the truth, that always works out. Not.

The food is standard coffee shop quality. Danny ate all of

his and everything I had left on my plate. I sucked down part of his shake and my soda. We enjoy the time out together, watching the people out roaming the casino at this hour and the tables around us in the coffee shop, who are mostly drunk trying to figure out where they want to go next.

Danny kisses my hand and leads me out of the coffee shop, back to our room. He's truly the sweetest ever. He kicks off his shoes and takes his clothes off. I take my bra off and he slides my shorts off. He likes me in his shirt and unties it, leaving it hanging long and baggy on me. He turns on the hard rock station with the volume low and turns off all the lights. He takes me in his arms and takes both of us to bed, pulling the blankets up over us and holding me against him while we fall asleep.

I wake up with my face against Danny's chest, one hand resting on his waist and the other touching Tiger. Danny's face is buried in my hair, one arm under my head with his hand leading to the small of my back, the other arm reaching over me and holding me close. Our legs are stretched out together and occupying the same space. We're still protected from the world, under the blankets with the music playing in the background. This is officially my favorite place to be. It's warm, and if everything else on the face of the earth suddenly went to shit, I wouldn't care because I'd still have Danny.

He squeezes me close and I nuzzle into him, pressing my lips to his chest and thinking about things I want to say to him, but can't. I want to tell him how much he means to me and it's a challenge. I can't explain it. I can't say anything serious or real to him without confessing first. I mean imagine this in perfect British accent, "You're so special to me. Nobody means as much as you do. I want to be with you forever." It doesn't work. When it's not even my real voice, how can the words be real? How can I be anything other than a joke? Danny takes me seriously, but I can't take myself seriously and it keeps taking me back to telling him the truth. But, I can't. It hurts in my chest when I consider it. It would end us. I stay exactly where I am without speaking, aware of the truth, and trying not to admit it to myself. I'm not falling. I already fell.

Danny kisses my head, "Jacks, baby, I want to hold you all day," he says softly. "I want to pretend you only belong to me."

The truth is I do. I only belong to him, but I can't say the words. "It sounds amazing. Tell me more."

"We'll stay in bed together all day. Listen to the radio and watch movies. Order room service. Be naked together. Snuggle under the blankets. I'll make you happy over and over, Jacks."

"I like the sound of that. I'm already happy just being here with you." I run my hand down his chest and outline his abs with my fingers.

"You make me happy, too." Then he shows me how happy I make him when he rolls to his back and turns our blanket cave into a tent. I giggle and he pulls me onto his chest, kissing me softly with his mouth closed and running his hands up and down my back under his shirt. He moves his hands down and squeezes my ass. Tiger's getting impatient.

"Are you making Tiger go after me or is he doing that by himself?"

"Tiger wants what I want. Just no self-control. When he wants it, he goes after it."

"Danny, are you holding back on me?" If Tiger wants me now then Danny must, too. "If you want me, why aren't you having me?"

"Jacks, it's not how this works. I can't keep having sex with you all the time, whenever I want."

"You can today." I press my lips to his and shove my tongue into his mouth with unforeseen desire. I play with his hair, running my fingers through the new length he's grown. I kiss him with need, and his body buzzes with happiness and desire. His hands are on Tiger. Tiger is after me, searching for my wet heat. I slide back a bit to find Tiger, moving on him slowly and taking him as I can. My hands are on Danny's chest and shoulders, holding on, bent over him. I'm overcome by how much I want more and I push until I've taken Tiger completely.

"Damn, Jacks. How are you doing this? You're so fucking perfect. How can you feel this perfect? You know what I want before I do," his breathing is already ragged.

It's because we belong together, but I can't say it. I keep moving on him, appreciating him and working his desire— things I can do, and hope he recognizes my heart. Slowly and silently I build intensity and bring him to climax. His body belongs to me in the moment, I own him.

"Jacks, oh baby." He places his hands on my hips, feeling me move on him. "Jacks. The way your hips move. Oh." His eyes are closed and he's simply appreciating me on him. "I've never had a girl take me this way and give up control. You're my first and my only. I'm only giving myself to you." His words hit me in the heart. I move on him faster and harder. If I'm the first and the only, he isn't going to forget it and I'm going to make sure it's a spectacular finish. I lean forward, sliding off of him as far as I can and I push back onto him, then I do it again. Driving noises from him I've never heard before, low moans of pleasure. The control is addictive and I want more. The whole time I'm getting closer. I toss the blankets back and sit up on Danny, grinding against him. He loves to be in me when I orgasm. I bounce on his long hard cock and start to drive myself out of my mind, when he reaches for me, lighting my skin on fire with his touch. He's exquisite, the way he stretches and fills me. I reach down to touch myself and meet his fingers with mine. I move his fingers on me, using him to get me off and I go quickly. Screaming out his name, he pulls me down to him and buries himself all the way inside me while he takes my lips with his. He falls over the edge while he's riding me through and I push him farther, not stopping, wanting him to have it all.

We're both spent and I'm collapsed on his chest with Tiger still inside me. Danny pulls the blankets back up over us and puts his loving arms around me, gently kissing my forehead. He holds me and we fall back to sleep.

I wake in the same position I fell asleep in, my head resting on Danny's chest. It's relaxing to listen to his heartbeat, and have him breathing underneath me. He rubs my back, he must've been awake before me. "Baby, let's stay right here."

The day was unforgettable. We watched movies in bed. We had sex. We ordered room service. We had more sex. We talked. We made out. We couldn't keep our hands off each other, and why would we? We made silly faces at each other like kids. We smiled and we laughed. Tiger and our connection is out of the ordinary, but the way he makes me laugh is what truly melts my heart.

———

I wake up Sunday morning early with Danny's arms around me and he only has a few hours until he needs to be at work. I slide down under the blankets and catch Tiger at rest. I kiss him and take him in my mouth, sucking on him lightly and he immediately comes alive. I grab him with both hands and lick him from end to end. Low sighs coming from Danny tell me he's appreciative. I kiss Tiger all over and stroke him with both hands, taking him in my mouth and humming vibrations around him.

Sucking and stroking him until he's rock hard. His hands are in my hair, feeling my head move on him. Sounds of pleasure come from his lips.

"Jacks, baby, you're the best." Danny starts to move his hips, wanting more. "I need you baby. Come here to me."

I keep stroking and sucking him, ignoring his request.

"Jacks, please. Please, I need you." Danny begs me. I keep going and he's tired of me ignoring him. He grabs me and pulls me to him. Pressing his lips to mine. "When I want you, I want you now and I need you. I need to feel you. I need to be buried in you." He rolls me under him and lies on top of me, kissing me hard, sucking my tongue, sucking my lips, biting my neck. Making me want him as much as he wants me in the moment. The urgency and desire are breathtaking. Being out of control and free, leaving myself in his hands, he'll please me like no other man. He wants me, needs me and he'll always protect me. Nobody else exists, it's only us. He explores me everywhere, feeling my smooth skin, he moves his hands down my body. Kissing a trail from my mouth to my breasts and back to my mouth. He pulls his mouth away from me and lets out a guttural groan when he starts to push into me. He pulls back and thrusts into me harder. "Oh, fuck me, you're so good. Oh, Jacks." Danny calls out my name and thrusts into me again and again. Kissing my neck turns to sucking my neck in just the right spot and he's got me going crazy. Crying out his name in need and moving my hips with him. My hands roam his body and caress every muscle as he takes me to the stars. I close my eyes and all I can do is revel in all that is Danny.

"You make me crazy. Please, Danny, more. You make me lose control." He's in control and I'm in a whole other land. I hear myself speak and don't even know what I'm saying until the words come out. "I need you, Danny. I want to stay with you. I don't want to leave you. I… anything for you." My words scare me, but spur Danny on and he claims my mouth passionately. He has no words, hanging on the edge of heaven and showing me we are in the same place. His kiss softens and slows, and his strokes do the same. But, our hearts are beating strong and the friction between us could generate enough power to light the Strip.

Out of nowhere his slow strokes send me to the moon, higher than ever before and he whispers in my ear, "It's only you for me, Jacks. Only you."

"Oh, Danny!" I call out his name. My heart fills and hurts at the same time. I should tell him the truth. Selfishly protecting my heart, I can't make myself tell him.

Danny increases his pace, I squeeze him uncontrollably and whimper at his every stroke. He goes off so hard I can feel him throbbing and he forgets to breathe. He gazes into my eyes as he comes, searching for something and showing me his heart, our future there.

CHAPTER NINETEEN

Dropping Danny off at work and driving home alone is one of the hardest things I've ever done. It wasn't a picnic for him either, but at least he has the distraction of having to work. He explained repeatedly to me how he doesn't want to wait a month before he sees me again, how we should be together. He wishes he could be with me every day. He misses me. He's honest and real, qualities becoming more evident the longer I'm with him and making it harder and harder to confess. I admire his values and have attempted to live the same way. The one time I wasn't doing anything wrong intentionally, ends up the time I do the most harm to myself, and even worse, I'll hurt the person who means the most to me. I fell and I'll lose the one man I'll ever fall for.

I try my drive home fast with the windows down and the music blaring routine, but all I do is cry. Every song makes me miss him, or think about him, or mad at myself, or has me questioning the L word.

My pager is vibrating with a 702 number before I get to the

state line. I pull off the freeway and call on the first pay phone I find.

"Hello?" and I hear the voice that makes me happiest.

"Hi, Danny. Is everything okay?" I speak, trying to maintain some normalcy and not let on that I've got tears running down my face.

"No. I miss you, Jacks. I need you. When will I see you again?" Danny's as bad as me. There needs to be a better way.

"How about Saturday? Even if you don't have a whole day off, I'll be there. I want to be with you, too." My heart flips at the idea.

"Okay, next weekend. Drive safe and I'll page you when I get home." I can hear the smile fill his voice and much more. "I have to get working. I'm always thinking about you," and he hangs up.

I continue my drive home and for the first time in months, there's no one waiting for me when I get home. There's no note on the door. There's no 2am house call. There's only me trying to get caught up on laundry, and a page from Danny. It's different, but not wrong. In fact, it's right.

Over the next few months I live the way I want to and I don't care about the world around me judging me. If I'm not happy, it's not worth it.

I go to work, get my job done, and exceed all expectations. Partly because I have a goal in mind, including gas money to get to Las Vegas.

Bryan has been scarce, only leaving me flyers for his gigs. Sometimes notes saying he wants me to show up for a specific gig. One time there was a longer note, but he scribbled it out and simply wrote, "You're still my friend."

Rob stopped by, but only because he wanted the clothes I'd stolen from him. Why did I keep his Pixies T-shirt in the first place? When he asked for his Jane's Addiction T-shirt, I pretended I didn't have a clue what he was talking about—I love that shirt. At least he finally got a clue.

Dot checks in on me a couple times per week, mostly to make sure somebody knows where I am. She doesn't want me lost in the middle of the desert. Also, any excuse to have margaritas and talk about sex is a good one. She hasn't asked if I've confessed yet, but she wants to. She doesn't want to know bad enough to risk cutting off the sexcapade stories.

Jess has been around some, but so busy with her new work contract that she can't focus on anything else. It's a good thing, otherwise she'd figure out what I'm doing and I'd never hear the end of it. I miss our crazy times, nobody does crazy like us. But, at least she's not judging me and giving me the mom look.

Danny. He pages me daily, usually at his break and after he gets home from work. He always has something sweet to say and always talks to me in his voice that makes my insides all fluttery. He sometimes includes something dirty, but usually more of an "I need you" in a horny way. I've been driving to Las Vegas every weekend. Sometimes I want him to come to me, but going to Danny keeps him compartmentalized from my non-British world and I love the long drive with the music blaring. My personal not so quiet time. About every three weeks we get lucky and Danny can get a whole weekend off. I've found if I leave for Vegas at about 1am, it gets me to his place in time to be in his bed with him a few hours and wake up with him wrapped around me on Saturday morning, or to pick him up from work when he works the over night shift. Mostly I hang out and find something to do, or bring whatever novel I'm reading at the time to keep busy while he's at work, and get to spend two nights with Danny or whatever time works with his schedule. But, admittedly, I've made a banzai run a couple times—including one Wednesday when I got off work and made it to Vegas in under three hours, spent an unforgettable night with Danny and drove back to get to work in time on Thursday morning and in the same clothes I left work in the day before—except for the T-shirt I stole from Danny while I was there, he shouldn't wear Neil Diamond anyway. We've been together at least weekly and the time apart isn't fun, the real world always gets in the way.

Okay. Fine. The thing that really gets in the way. The real reason we're where we are. It's why our relationship hasn't moved forward. It's why I can't tell him how much he means to me and what I dream about. What I'm afraid can only be a dream. It's why we've fallen into this pattern of me driving to Vegas and returning pages. It all goes back to the first word I said to him and the word itself doesn't even matter. What matters is how I said it. What matters even more is how I continue to say things to him the same way. It's the British accent. I have a second life playing the part of a British chick, but I want her life to be mine. I want her man, I mean my man.

CHAPTER TWENTY

I'll never forget the last time I saw Danny. Jess was with me on the trip to Vegas and we had a room at the Excalibur, it was still one of the newer hotels and cheap to boot. The relationship with Danny had been going on for over six months and I could make the drive to Las Vegas in my sleep. Jess was there on purpose and she was determined to make a point, in hindsight I wish she'd done it sooner. She figured out I was making trips to Vegas often and I told her I bought a pager. Every time my pager went off I radiated enough happiness to light a city. She grabbed my pager, saw the 702 and immediately went into a rant about guys in Vegas being only for fun. Then she specifically asked if it was Danny and how far things had gotten between us. Rather than hiding it, I laid it all out there because she'd be the one who picked up my pieces, if anybody did. Besides, if nothing else, I've learned never to lie. Jess found out I was still using the British accent with him and hadn't told him the truth, she booked a room, told me we were going to Vegas and I was telling him. Period. I was horrified. Yes, I'd considered it numerous times and in my heart I knew it needed to be done. Danny held my happiness, my pleasure, and my heart. I'd become accustomed to his face and his body. I lived the lie, so I could keep him even though it was limiting where we could grow to as a couple. I lied to myself and convinced myself it was the best thing to do, but honestly, I was scared and I shouldn't have been.

Danny met me at the Excalibur and was surprised I wasn't alone, Jess was with me. He knew I had a room, it wasn't the first time we'd gotten a room at the Excalibur. Jess turned to me sternly after observing our interaction, "Do it now. Handle business and get it over with. I'll be up in two hours if I haven't heard from you," and she walked away.

"That's a good idea, let's go up to the room and talk," Danny put his arm around me and held me close on our way to the room.

Something is wrong. Danny's still treating me the same and looking at me the same way. He's happy to be here with me and he still wants me, but seems nervous. I wonder if Jess called him and told him already.

I unlock the room and we sit on the bed together. Danny reaches for me and kisses me like I'm his last breath, then pushes away. "I need to talk to you and I'm sorry. I want you to know I'd always choose you. This is all my fault and I'm sorry. I'd hoped we could be together, just us, always. We were getting closer to being us." What the fuck is going on here? I'm missing something. What's he rambling about? "I'm not making this up, or trying to get rid of you." Trying to get rid of me? Hold on. This can't be real. Is he dumping me? "Please listen to me." What's he so worried about? "I accidentally got my co-worker pregnant and we're moving in to an apartment together, I'm taking you there to show you this afternoon. I have to do the right thing. It's my baby and I will take care of it, it's the only thing that could ever take me from you. A bunch of us got together and partied after a bad shift at work, we all got drunk, and shit happened. Honestly, I don't even remember having sex."

You'd think I'd be upset about him having sex with another girl, but I wasn't. Thinking back, I should've been. I never even considered he might cheat on me, but then again we didn't have that kind of relationship because I refused to go there with my lie. I was in shock and simply, numb.

"It was never that way with you. I always knew what I was doing and I knew the risks when I was taking them. A condom breaking with you would've been the best thing to ever happen to me. I love you, Jacks."

And there it was, the words every girl wants to hear from the right guy as part of his I-fucked-up-and-have-to-say-goodbye.

Somehow I'm not in tears. No better time than the present to say my piece. "Danny, I have something to tell you, too. I should've told you the night we met. I was scared it would end us, but I guess it doesn't matter anymore." He moves toward me and I gesture for him to stay where he is, keeping some distance between us. I drop the accent, "Danny, I've never been out of the United States. I'm not British. I was born and raised in LA. I'm a third generation California Girl."

Danny stares at me stunned, "Are you fucking kidding me? I've always wanted a California Girl, that's so much cooler than British. It just makes you hotter."

Seriously?

He didn't even care. He still wanted me and needed me—it didn't change anything. In fact, he wanted me more. But, he had to be an adult, a responsible father and we were over. I hate the word over.

I could've gotten him to move to LA with me, or I could've moved to Las Vegas. But, it's too late and the opportunity has passed. If I'd told him sooner… If I was permanent, not leaving for Europe at any moment—maybe the jokes about marrying me in Vegas to keep me in the country, so he could keep me here, would've been closer to our real life. Maybe I would've been able to tell him I love him because there wouldn't have been a lie between us.

"I don't want to see the place you're going to live with her and have your family. I don't want to hear her name and I don't want to know what she looks like. I'm sure you'll be happy." Anger suddenly comes bursting out of me, but mostly I was mad at myself. "I'm sorry, I have no right to say that. I'm the one who has been lying to you for months."

"Jacks, you have every right. You were afraid to tell me you weren't British because you didn't want to lose me. I was stupid, got drunk, and knocked up my co-worker. I'll have the happiness of my child, but I won't be happy without you. Nothing is the same without you."

"Everything else has always been me." I'm emphatic with my words, wanting him to know it was always me without question. "I didn't hide myself from you. I've always shown you my real personality, my real feelings and I've never faked anything except my voice. The night I met you the accent was innocent enough, it was a homework assignment." My sadness is overwhelming and he insists on showing me where he's moving to.

It would never be the same, I felt it in the weakening beat of my heart. I'd probably never see Danny again, and if I did we wouldn't be able to be us. He'd never asked me to drive to Vegas again, I'm sure he felt like he shouldn't. He always did what he considered morally right. I'm the one who wasn't so clear on doing the right thing. The sad thing is, I still would've been there in a heartbeat even if I had to call in sick. We never got to be together without my lie. I was always British. I never got to be his California Girl. It still makes my heart hurt, he always wanted a California Girl—well, fuck me.

For months, Danny still called me. At first, it was still every day and I gave him my direct number at work and home. No reason to hide anything. It got harder for him to get phone time. He was trying to hide me from the other woman. Or, maybe I'm the other woman, but I was here first! It got harder to talk for both of us, even though it made me happy to hear his voice. I'd end up in tears at the end of most days, thinking about us and blaming myself. Our contact slowly dwindled to weekly and less and less, until he was gone.

The day I received the generic Las Vegas postcard in the mail, I lost hope. The postcard itself doesn't matter. There was no name or return address on it. The words written on the back are what have been engrained in my brain since the day I read them, "Live your dreams and you'll be in mine." I run my fingers along the ink he left on the card. Simple words that are anything but simple to my heart. I grab my photo strip from under my pillow, gazing at the photo of his handsome face and us together. The way he focused on me, his admiration is undeniable. Hot tears flow down my cheeks and my chest hurts. It's over. I fucking hate the word over.

———

I did my best to throw myself into work. Dot made a point of making me go out for shopping therapy and Jess was dragging me out almost every weekend trying to get me laid, or as she so eloquently put it, "Fuck that guy right out of your head."

Bryan continued to leave me flyers for his gigs and after catching me at home a couple weekends in a row, knocked instead of taping his flyer to my door. I was torn, not wanting to talk to anybody and having not talked to or seen him in months. But, I answered the door. "Hey, come on in."

Bryan blinked at me surprised and walked in, guitar in hand. He didn't ask any questions, he simply said, "It'd be great if you came to my gig this weekend. I want your feedback on the changes my band has made. Do you want to hear the new stuff I've written?" He looked at me earnestly, waiting for a response and not proceeding until he got one.

"Jess wants to go out this weekend, I'll tell her. I'm sure she'll be in."

"Cool. I'll put you on the list, so you don't have to pay the cover." Bryan smiles at me, aware that Jess and I never pay the cover.

"So, tell me what you've been writing." It's nice to have a visitor and if nothing else, music is my favorite distraction.

Bryan doesn't speak, he simply starts strumming on his guitar and singing. Song after song. Some traditional Bryan style, overly emotional my girl left me or dirty fuck me songs. Others with a deeper pain of cheating and being betrayed, being left alone in love, finding love when it wasn't expected and simply missing someone. His voice holds a sincere and meaningful tone, while his fingers play like they're driven by another force. He'd improved his game and it's impressive because he had game before. After about eight songs, he stops and turns to me for a reaction.

"Wow! I've never heard you so, wow. Good songs. Real emotion. Fantastic, Bryan." I mean every word of it, he's a true musician.

He hugs me, "Thanks. I gotta go. I'm late for practice," and he's gone.

I call Jess and tell her about the gig, and even though Bryan isn't her favorite she's encouraged that I actually want to go out and she won't have to drag me kicking and screaming.

Jess picks me up Saturday and takes me out to dinner before going to the gig. Not our normal night out. She's checking on me, trying to figure out where my head is and possibly my heart. She seems satisfied when I suggest we hit a different club where the band starts earlier first, then go to Bryan's gig. But, she doesn't go for it because she wants to drink, or I should say, she wants to get me drunk and the place Bryan is gigging is the best place to drink more than you should. We were on our third cocktail and had been doing shots before the band even started. We got there early and he'd been watching me. He even walked up to Jess and said something to her, but I couldn't hear him. Jess simply gave him a nod.

The band sounds tight. They've all stepped up their game. Bryan doesn't have any women hanging on him, he isn't even talking to any of the ladies who are trying. He walks away from them. Between sets he walks over to our table, flips a chair around and sits straddling it with a cup of hot tea. I've never seen him this way at a gig before and I've been to plenty of his shows. There have always been women.

At the end of the night, Bryan talks into the mic, "We're going to do a little something different tonight. Ending with a new song I wrote. I hope you'll enjoy it and have a great night. This one's for you, Jackie." He starts to pick at his acoustic guitar, the most beautiful solo with his rhythm guitarist adding some soft depth in the background. He changes to a patterned strum with chords and sings:

Everything happens for a reason
I needed to open my eyes to see
Bad timing is what saved me
Showed me what you mean to me
Now I need to give you pleasin'

You can forget about him
I'm all you'll ever need
Please forget about him
Give me a chance and you'll see

I know I didn't treat you right
You deserve to be the only one
I was always looking just for fun
Now I gravitate around your sun
And I'm ready to put up a fight

You can forget about him
I'm all you'll ever need
Please forget about him
Give me a chance and you'll see

I've always been your friend
Now I stand beside you asking for more
I've sent all the others out the door
It's only you that I adore
Can we be together until the end

You can forget about him
I'm all you'll ever need
Please forget about him
Give me a chance and you'll see

Please let me make you smile
I can wash away your sad
It won't be like what we had
Baby, you're driving me mad
Jackie, I'll make it worthwhile

You can forget about him
I'm all you'll ever need
Please forget about him
Give me a chance and you'll see

I hope I'm not too late
I know you're all I need

You can forget about him
I'm all you'll ever need

Oh, Jackie
Give me a chance and you'll see

He plays out the song, finishing with a fade of picking similar to the beginning. The song is beautiful and I'm stunned. I was sure he'd given up on me and moved on to his old ways, but it's obvious he hasn't. I'm not ready. He's looking at me and I smile, wave, and run out of the bar with Jess not far behind me. Yep, that's how I'm playing it. I can't face him. In fact, I'm staying at Jess's place tonight. I can't be trusted.

The next day, I call Bryan and get lucky when his voicemail picks up, "The band was great last night. You were amazing. The last song was unexpected and beyond words—which is saying a lot coming from me. I'm sorry I ran out. I didn't know you were waiting for me. I thought you'd given up on me and I wouldn't blame you if you had. My wounds are too fresh and I'm not ready. I'm sorry, Bryan. You're great," and I hang up.

Bryan hangs out and comes by my place weekly to play and sing like he always has. It has been a year to the day since I'd heard from Danny and I was fit to be tied. My emotions were controlling me. Bryan shows up with his guitar and immediately recognizes that I'm not right. He leaves and comes back with a bottle of Jack and two shot glasses. He kisses me and it makes me feel something. My heart isn't dead. It's broken into smithereens and still bleeding. "I know he's still in there, but let me try to get rid of him," Bryan says and I agree. Bryan tried the same thing about once a month and I let him, but it was never the same as it was before. Never wanting him. Always him wanting me. Never the heat and emotion I could only get from Danny.

CHAPTER TWENTY-ONE

Every time I drive into Las Vegas I remember my time with Danny vividly. I've even driven by the no-tell motel he lived in and I spent many nights at with him. I've wandered through casinos hoping I might accidentally run into him and somehow convince him he still needs me, as if he still lived in Vegas and I don't know that he does. Sometimes I miss him more than anybody else could ever understand. I understand why he did what he did and I honor him for it. It doesn't mean I have to like it and I'm sure he doesn't either. Danny's such a stand-up guy, always doing the right thing. I wish he wouldn't have been that time, but it's part of his make-up and that's part of what makes him special. It's why I miss him. He was the one, and he'll always be the one I compare others to. He's why I'll always be single. When I'm comparing, nobody comes close to Danny. We weren't exclusive and it didn't matter because we were us, nobody else mattered. The distance was the problem, but by the time my secret was out and we knew what our real options were—we could be together—it was too late and it was my fault. I suppose I started it with a lie and it timed out with his mistake. We all make mistakes.

You're thinking it wasn't my fault. I didn't party with my co-workers and get wasted into oblivion. I didn't get knocked up by another guy. Danny partied, fucked his co-worker, and got her pregnant. But, you're wrong. If I wasn't scared. If I was honest and told him the truth in the beginning or even on one of my first couple visits—we'd still be together. It's true. He wouldn't have been out partying. He might have knocked me up instead, but we'd still be together. He might have moved to LA or I might be living in Las Vegas. We would still be together. I did this to myself. I did this to Danny. If I'd told him the truth, I would've been able to tell him how much I want to be with him. I'll always love him and I've never told him. He'll always be my happy.

CHAPTER TWENTY-TWO

One thing I've learned to do is live my life and not give up on my dreams. I've been pursuing my music career, doing auditions, sending out introductions with recordings to studios and producers, putting myself out there and searching for my opportunity. I'm confident I can sing lead, but I'd be ecstatic to get a chance at studio work as a background singer. I've been to countless auditions around Hollywood and LA, but I'm one of zillions hoping for my break and the best I've gotten is a "we'll call you" and playing with a couple of local bands that wanted to add female vocals to their sound. Singing with the bands was fun, but not worth the drama with Bryan when the band members were hitting on me.

Yes, Bryan is still around. Like I said before, I've always thought we'd end up together. Funny thing is he wants me and I don't want him the way I did before. Even Bryan doesn't compare to Danny and every time I'm with Bryan I have Danny's voice in my ear telling me to remember him. But, a girl needs attention, and I've allowed it to be Bryan. Nobody else since Danny, only Bryan. You might think it sounds like a long-term relationship and it is, but not in a positive way. I'm just not interested. You may accuse me of being scared, and to some extent you'd be right, but it's not what you assume. I'm not scared to put my heart out there. I'm scared the only person worthy of picking it up and holding it is out of my life forever and I'll never have another chance to be with him again. Truth is, I'm sure of it. There's a loss and emptiness in my heart. I remind myself of it everyday, not intentionally. Something happens and throws it in my face while I'm going about my daily routine. There hasn't been contact from Danny in a long time and I understand the phone conversations were making it hard. We both wanted the same thing and we couldn't have it. It just drew out the pain. It was hard on both of us, though I do wish I had some type of automated update system with a monthly newsletter about him.

The problem with Bryan is he gets jealous of me gigging and the guys in the bands I've played with. He gets upset when I miss him playing because I have a gig or an audition. He's still selfish, even though he has learned to be more giving in other ways. He's caught on to what I want from a man and he tries, sometimes he achieves it for short periods of time. Most importantly, he's not Danny and he never will be.

I've started traveling for auditions. Maybe it's true, you need to be in the right place at the right time. Lightning striking in a positive way. I need to find the right place. This has been a challenge because I still have to work, but I'm doing my best to manage more out of town chances. I took Monday and Tuesday off, so I could have a long weekend and do a handful of auditions in Las Vegas. It's an easy trip and the stars aligned with how the audition opportunities are scheduled. You might think Vegas? Yes, Vegas. There are openings in lounge acts and bands, some need back-ups to cover the off days, some need new lead singers or want a new piece to liven up the show. Most of the resorts have full production shows now, too. Musicals, tributes, look-alikes, sound-alikes, the list goes on and on. Vegas was a special place for me in the past, maybe it's where I belong. Or, maybe I can get a second job and sing on the weekends. Sometimes it takes baby steps.

This weekend I'm checked into the Excalibur by myself and prepared to knock it out of the park at my auditions. Singing with the bands has allowed me to get more experience and build my power. Even the guys who work in the warehouse have mentioned it's different hearing me sing when I wander the stacks, before they heard noise and thought I was talking to myself.

It's been four years since the last time I was in Las Vegas. I've told myself I'm not going to let my location get to me this weekend, no wandering the Danny hot spots—but, I probably will. It's hard when my auditions are all over town and I've been all over town with Danny.

My first audition is at the Stardust. They're looking for a few people to do solo performances with the house band in a supper club setting with dancing. It sounds fun and it's a chance to do something a bit different. The production team is tasting food in between auditions. They must still be working on the menu. I walk out on stage ready to sing and the crew calls out to the chef bringing the samples out, "Hey Danny! We want to try some of that. Bring some out for us, too." Danny? I scan the room and sure enough—Danny.

It's inappropriate behavior, but I need him to know I'm in the room, "Danny, me too."

He searches the room and finds me on the stage. "Jacks?" He yells across the room.

Hearing him call my name in the questioning tone, but

hopeful, catches me off guard. Nobody has called me Jacks in years. It's only ever been Danny. "In the flesh." Bad choice of words, he turns red and I feel need, a need to touch his flesh.

"Jackie, we're ready to hear you," the director calls out.

"I've prepared 'Get Here' by Oleta Adams." I nod to the stage-hand to play the music. I notice Danny stays to listen and watch my audition. I hope the shock of his unexpected presence doesn't throw me off. My heart is beating stronger and faster than normal. He's here. He's okay. He's still in Vegas. I start to sing and there's more emotion flowing through me than I've experienced in years, especially when I hit the last lines of the chorus—I need you closer. The tone and emotion conveyed by the song are already deep without Danny. It's all I can do to maintain my composure. I break the unwritten performance rules by closing my eyes at one point and by focusing on Danny for the couple of lines. Danny gives me a thumbs up and gestures to me, he'll meet me outside when I'm done. After that, I don't even hear everything the director says.

"Great song choice, it would fit in perfectly in a supper club. We'd like to hear something you perform regularly, whatever genre it may be."

"Okay, most of my live experience has been rock with a live band." I turn to the stage-hand, "Please cue up track 7 and if you can turn it up a bit, I take this one loud." I turn back to the director. "This is 'Crazy' by Aerosmith." He asked for it, I bet he hasn't heard anything like this in here today. Could be the wrong move for the audition, but they say you should give the directors and casting what they ask for. I'm not holding back and this will give me a chance to show my range, my timing abilities, and my live stage skills. Danny's walking out when the music starts, but stops when he hears my vocals. I love how he can't help himself. I hit it full on with intensity, the whole way from the beginning to the end.

"You've got some great diversity and skill there. Please check back with us in a couple of hours." Sounds like a call back to me.

"Thank you." I walk off stage and Danny's at the door in the back motioning for me to follow him. Something happens I never expected, I hesitate. Am I going to go where he asks? Follow after him when he quit calling? Yes. I follow Danny out of the room and I'm not sure what to expect, he's at work.

"Jacks, I can't believe you're here. You sounded great in there and you look better than I remembered." Danny keeps his distance. He did knock-up his co-worker, and this is his work.

"Thanks. I'm happy to see you. The chef's coat suits you." I try to keep it cool. I have no idea where this is going or what his current status is.

His melting brown eyes see right through me, "I've missed you, Jacks." Then why hasn't he called me? Paged me? Sent a letter via pigeon courier?

"I've missed you, too. I worried when you quit calling."

He cuts me off, "I don't have much time right now. I want to talk with you. Can we get together later or tomorrow?" I can tell there is some urgency.

"Sure. I'll be hanging out here for a couple of hours and I'm staying at Excalibur." I smile at him, on the verge of offering an invitation.

"Excalibur, some things don't change. I'd love to talk and I'm having a hard time keeping my hands off of you, but I'm being watched. I'm off at 6pm, if I can't find you here I'll leave you a message at your hotel."

"Room 821." I can't help myself, if I had an extra room key I would've given it to him. Danny heads off to get back to work and I'm left leaning on the wall, flooded by memories of our time together. I'm taken back to the warmth of his hands on my body and his soft lips against mine. I can taste the Midori and whiskey on his tongue, and my crazy need for him flutters low in my belly. I close my eyes and I'm suddenly in the darkness, hearing his ragged breaths, our bodies moving together, his breath warm at my ear, he's calling out my name, he needs me. I remember the fireworks exploding and the darkness taking over, all I could feel was him—and it's all I want. I'm taken over by the sensation of him, us together. Except, I want to show him what he means to me and make him understand with my actions, like he did for me. I never gave him that.

CHAPTER TWENTY-THREE

L ater in the evening I'm relaxing in my room. The day went well. The director was impressed with me and said they'll be calling me in the next week to make me an offer. It doesn't mean it'll be a good offer, but anything will be a step in the right direction. The room phone rings…

"Hello?" I answer.

"Hi, I had to stay at work late tonight. I was hoping to get out and see you, but I can't get out tonight. I have my daughter tonight. Do you have time to talk?" Danny explains himself somewhat nervously.

"That's a good idea. We can catch up. Where's your wife?" The question slips out before I can stop myself.

"Now, that sounds like my Jacks. I didn't marry her. I couldn't do it, I don't love her. I live with her, I play the part, and I do my part to take care of my family. I love my daughter and we make it work."

"I've decided to stay single, it's easier. The guys out there don't deserve me." Doing my best to stay focused and not lose it completely. He's not married! Did he just call me "my Jacks"?

I love it when he calls me Jacks. Nobody has called me Jacks in years, it was always only Danny.

"How about me?" he asks sincerely.

"It doesn't even matter. It's not an option. You're taken."

"I haven't touched her or any other girl since I moved in with her. Tiger has been pissed about it." He actually laughs about it. "I make it look like we're together. I don't want to embarrass her and I want to keep everything good for my daughter. She's out partying somewhere tonight. Can you meet me for lunch tomorrow?"

"I can meet you. I don't have any auditions tomorrow."

"I'll call you in the morning with a plan. Before we get together, I want you to know this is hard. I don't think I can act on it, but it's always only been you for me. Are you going home tomorrow?"

"I'm here until late Tuesday. I'm here alone. Maybe you deserve some selfish happiness and release." I should keep my mouth shut, but I can't help myself.

"Jacks, that's not a good idea." I can hear him shaking his head.

"You're not married. I'm not asking you to be my boyfriend or anything. I just want to spend some time alone with you. It makes me happy that you didn't marry her. Tiger shouldn't have to suffer." I smile at the imagery of us together that's suddenly running through my head.

Danny takes a deep breath, "I don't know if I can do that. I want to. I want you. Damn, I'd be happy just to hold your hand or kiss you. But, it's not fair to you for me to hide you. Like you said, you deserve better."

Do I want to be with him, if I'm a secret? Secrets are an interesting thing. Sometimes they make things more exciting, and other times they hide things and hurt people. Sometimes hiding the truth is allowing someone to lie. Huh, I've experienced what lying can do and I won't do it again. Hiding me to protect his family façade? That's not Danny. He'd never lie, it's not in him. He's fighting with his honor and seeing me has his desire in the lead. "Danny, I don't want to make you uncomfortable. Maybe we shouldn't meet. I get it, it's too hard having any contact with each other and keeping up your family life."

"No, I want to see you. It's important to me."

"Is she seeing anybody else? I mean, you said she's out partying." I ask and I probably shouldn't.

"I don't know. I don't ask. It doesn't matter to me."

"Then why should it matter to her if you're with somebody?" What do I have to lose?

"She knows you're the reason I won't be with her and commit to her, Jacks. If she finds out I'm with you, the arrangement will change and I don't know what she'll do."

Wait, can we rewind that last part please? It's been years since he's even talked to me and he's... "Danny, I'm fine with being your secret. I'm not here often. It could be months before I'm in Vegas again. But, I don't want you to risk what you have for me, your..." and I'm interrupted by something, someone who wants Danny's attention.

There's a shuffling sound in the background, "Daddy, can we watch cartoons?" The sweetest young voice has his attention.

"Yes, you go pick which one and I'll be out to watch with you in a minute. Okay, my angel?" Danny's voice is different than I've ever heard it, so sweet it makes me ache.

"Okay. Old cartoons or new cartoons?" she asks him.

"I like the old cartoons better."

"Okay, Daddy. I'm go pick." She shuffles off, with the

sound of something dragging and I can only imagine his daughter with her blanket or teddy bear.

"Sorry, she fell asleep in front of the TV and I thought she was out for the night."

"I understand," and boy do I understand. I can't mess this up for him. She's his everything. "Danny, you're doing the right thing. Don't risk it. Your daughter needs you. I'm a big girl and I can take care of myself."

"If I had my way, I'd take care of both of you," Danny still has his I-mean-it tone and he directs it at me. "I'll call in the morning and let you know about lunch. I need to go, she's getting antsy." He calls out to her in the background, letting her know he's going to be there in a minute. Then I hear the inno-cent giggle of his child. "It makes me happy to see you and talk to you, Jacks. Goodnight," and he hangs up.

I love hearing his voice, but it was unexpected. The reality of his life and his daughter, it never sunk in until now. Danny's a dad and it sounds like he's a good one. The sweet voice came from his daughter and she obviously worships him. Who wouldn't?

CHAPTER TWENTY-FOUR

I stayed out late Saturday night, checking out the lounge acts playing at the different casinos along the strip. I didn't plan on drinking, but it turns out last night was one of those Midori and Sprite nights. Some of the lounges had drink minimums and it's a light drink, so it worked well. I'm not talking about the fact Midori and Sprite is my Danny drink and always makes me smile. I met some of the bands and lounge acts, tried to get some information and gave them my number. A couple of them had me up on stage to sing lead on a song. Overall, it was a productive night getting noticed and making contacts, I'm getting somewhere.

Sunday morning the phone wakes me up at 10am. 10am is way too early when you didn't get back to your room until after 4am. "Hello?" I answer groggily.

"That's the sound of my sleepy Jacks. Good morning." Danny's voice comes through clear. I smile at "my sleepy Jacks," all is not lost and my undying hope is fueled.

"Good morning, I think," not having opened my eyes yet.

I've never been a morning person. When Danny and I spent time together, he wasn't a morning person either. Then again it could be because we were always up all night.

"Can you meet me at the Circus Circus arcade about 12:30? I'll be there when you get there, come find me."

"Sure, I'll see you then."

"Jacks, set an alarm or something. I know how you are in bed." Danny's tone sounds like sex on a stick when he says "in bed". It was on purpose and for my benefit. Sadly, it's all it takes to get my engine revved.

"I want to see you, Danny. I'll be there," and I hang up.

I stay in bed awhile longer before I get up to get ready. I spend as long as possible under the hot shower, then I pull on my tight jeans and a snug fitting Guns N' Roses T-shirt with my bulky Reebok high tops. I stand in the bathroom in front of the mirror fixing my hair, so it's all curled and fluffy. I shove some money, my driver's license, and my keys in my pocket, and head downstairs to my truck. I drive to the other end of the strip to find Circus Circus and park without any trouble. I remember playing air hockey with Danny here, and the photo booth we made out in. I never liked this place until he brought me here and showed me how much fun it could be. To be fair, Danny's the fun and it has nothing to do with the location. I walk into the casino and make my way through the crowds to find the arcade. It's 12:35, I'm running a few minutes late and I need to find Danny in this sea of people.

I spot Danny across the room and he's not alone. He's talking to someone and he picks up the person he's talking to, putting her on his shoulders. She's absolutely adorable and has his features, the same brown eyes, blonde hair, nose, mouth, all touched with femininity. My stomach sinks and my instinct to run is trying to take over at the moment Danny spots me and waves me over. There's no backing out now, I walk over to him and he pretends he's running into me accidentally.

"Hey! I haven't seen you in a long time," he reaches to shake my hand, slyly handing me a small note he doesn't want to get noticed. I read it in my palm without giving it away:

She didn't come home yet, so I brought my daughter with me. It will be fine, follow my lead.

Danny looks at his daughter and says, "Jackie, this is my friend Jacks." Danny searches my eyes waiting for my response. I'm sure he's wondering how I'll respond to his daughter having my name.

I study her sweet face, "Jackie is a pretty name. Where did it come from?" I ask her.

"Daddy says it's his favorite girl name," she answers, smiling and scrunching her nose. "Your name is Jacks? That's a funny name."

"Yes, Jacks is my name. It does sound a little funny." I giggle back at the girl with my name.

"Daddy, can I have ice cream?" she looks at him with these eyes that there's no way he says no to.

"I love ice cream," I say.

"Daddy, can Jacks have ice cream?" Jackie smiles at me proud of herself. Look what I did! I'm getting us both ice cream!

Danny watches our conversation and his happiness grows as we walk to the ice cream. He buys two ice cream cones, one he shares with Jackie and one for me. Mine is melting before he hands it to me, so he gazes into my eyes and gives it a big lick for my benefit. Making some comment about wanting to try the flavor. I go straight for the part he licked, trying to get as close to kissing him as I can and his eyes warm. I accidentally on purpose graze against him numerous times while we walk through the crowd, watching the circus around us.

"Okay my angel, we need to go home because you need a nap." Danny tells her in a way so he's sharing with me too. Then he mouths to me, "I want to be with you. I need to see you alone. I'll call you." He walks off with his precious load on his shoulders.

Still tired from last night, I go back to my room and nap. Before I lay my head down on the pillow, the phone rings, "Hello?"

"Hi, she's sleeping and I went for luck that you might be at your room."

"She's beautiful, Danny."

"You are, too. More beautiful every time I see you."

"I can't believe you named her Jackie."

"Her mom doesn't know where her name comes from, she doesn't know what your name is. She only knows what you look like because she saw my photo booth strip."

"She still hasn't come home from partying last night. She's done this before and shows up in the evening. I don't have work until noon tomorrow. Would it be okay with you if I go to your room after she gets home?"

"I don't know if it's a good idea. But, you're always welcome."

"It's a bad idea, and I want to do it anyway, even if I only get to see you this once."

"I'll have a key left for you at the front desk. Danny, don't take any chances with your girl." I hang up and call down to the front desk, having the key left for Danny. Then I lay down to nap, but I'm anxious. I switch gears and review my audition details and what I'll be performing when. I sing through each of the songs. Then I crash out exhausted, mentally and emotionally.

CHAPTER TWENTY-FIVE

I wake up a few hours later starving, having only had ice cream today. I need to go find food. I get up, turn on the Vegas hard rock station, wash my face, and brush out my hair before I head down to the casino in search of something to satisfy my belly. I take the elevator down to the casino and stay right where I am when Danny is standing there waiting for the elevator doors to part. He smiles at me and joins me in the elevator with his duffle bag over his shoulder. This is the first time we've been alone together in years, since the day he told me about her and I confessed my lie. The day he told me he loved me. The thought makes me reach my arms around his neck and hug him tightly, wishing I'd never have to let go.

Danny slides his arm around my waist and buries his face in my hair, "I've missed you so much, Jacks. Your arms around me are a dream come true." I can't speak and I can't let go. The elevator doors open, forcing me to move, and Danny holds my hand as we walk to my room. I unlock the door and he follows me in, setting down his bag and taking something out. "Where were you going?"

"I was going to find food," Maybe I should order room service.

"Good, you're hungry. I brought dinner." Danny proceeds to open up containers as he pulls them from his bag. He's prepared. He has Midori and Sprite, which he puts in the mini-fridge with another small container. The spread he unloads on the table is crazy. A whole bunch of things in small portions. "I've been working on recipes all afternoon and I hoped you might want to try some." Did he say he made all of this tempting looking food? The smell of it alone is making my tummy rumble. Does somebody hate me? How can Danny be better than perfect? Well, perfect other than the fact that we can't be together. There's pasta with white sauce, pasta with red sauce, fresh bread, citrus marinated chicken, bacon cheeseburger sliders, green salad with herbs dressed in balsamic vinaigrette, pulled pork macaroni and cheese, and this bag he's keeping from me, refusing to open—dessert. I can smell the chocolate and peanut butter. He opens each of the containers and tells me about the process, "I enjoy cooking and creating recipes. I've been trying updates on the recipes I use most often. Tony is fat," he laughs out loud. "I hope you like it."

"It smells yummy." My eyes widen with anticipation.

Danny twirls some of the pasta with red sauce onto a fork and feeds me, watching for my reaction. Then he forks a piece of the chicken and eats it, before feeding a piece to me. He puts together the perfect bite of salad and rubs it against the side of the container to pick up more of the dressing, continuing to feed me. He pokes a few pieces of penne pasta with the white sauce. Then he cuts a slider in half, followed by the mac and cheese—everything as tasty as what came before it, or better. Danny's eyes are gleaming, he knows I love all of it. "Danny, this is all so delicious," I say with my mouth full and grab the container of the mac and cheese.

Danny laughs, "I guess all Jackies like my pulled pork mac and cheese. Jackie calls it piggy mac."

"She's a smart girl. She's lucky to have you. Your food is amazing." I'm impressed and I continue to shove food into my mouth.

"Thanks, Jacks." He turns to me happy with himself, but torn. He closes his eyes and opens them slowly. "I'm not here to have sex. I miss having you with me, hanging out, and having fun the most. I miss your laugh and the smell of your hair. I miss waking up with my arms around you, holding you cuddled to my chest. I miss you singing to the radio. I miss you stealing my clothes. I miss how free and loving you are with me, always one of the things I liked about you most. I had no idea how special it was and how much I need it in my life. I need you and I'll take whatever little bit of you I can get. Seeing you makes me remember how happy I can be."

"You're better than me. I want you selfishly, all to myself, and I want all of you. But, I'll do whatever it takes to help you keep her happy and Jackie safe."

"She gave me my daughter, but I'm tired of keeping her happy. It's my turn to be happy. She hates you because I don't look at her the way I looked at you in the photo booth, and it makes her mad because Jackie doesn't look like her at all. She actually thinks Jackie resembles you more than her and we'd look more like a family, all being blondes. I'm telling you, she's out of her mind. There's nothing that would make me happier than having both of my girls with me, living in the same home. I guess that's a different dream, maybe someday."

I listen and I let him vent, but all I can focus on is how

badly I want him and tonight can't be about sex unless he wants it to be. It's an odd turn. I can't remember Danny ever not wanting sex. "I don't want to overstep my boundaries and I want to kiss you, but that can lead to other things. I wish I could make your dream come true. How can I make you happy tonight?"

Danny pops half a slider into his mouth while he closes up the food. Then he pulls his T-shirt off, unleashing his tiger tattoo that's always my undoing and pulls me to the bed with him. He carefully pulls my shirt off over my head. He unbuttons my jeans and pushes them off, leaving me standing there in my bra and panties. He pulls the blankets back and climbs into my bed, holding the blankets up for me to join him. I crawl into bed next to him and he covers us up in our own private cocoon, putting his arms around me and simply appreciating my presence. He runs his hands along my body, feeling my skin and igniting his memory. "It's not living when I don't have you near me," he whispers quietly to me.

His words are too much for me and I can't hold back. I press my lips to the closest part of him I can reach, his chest. "Jacks, do you need me?" unsure of what he's doing and where he stands.

"Yes. I need you every day. I miss you and I miss the way you make me feel. Right now, being close to you this way is making me want to touch you and kiss you all over. I want you to remember me. I want you to be happy. I, I don't want you to hold back. The last time we were alone you told me you loved me and I want you to show me, I want to feel how much you love me." What am I saying? Don't add pressure on him. Keep it light and make him happy. I need to give him an out. Fuck, I don't want to give him an out—I want to keep him. "But, I don't want to make this any harder on you and I understand it might be better for you to leave right now and never talk to me, never see me again." The tears are welling up in my eyes and I can taste their saltiness.

Danny tightens his arms around me, "I remember everything about you, Jacks. Nobody can take your memory away from me. Just having you in my arms makes me happy." He kisses my head sweetly and I wait for more.

A few hours later, around midnight I wake up and find I fell asleep in his arms. I'm shook up when I wake up with someone in bed with me, and I must be dreaming because it's Danny. I quietly sneak off to the bathroom, trying not to disturb him. But when I return he's sitting up and awake. I take off my bra and my panties. Danny gazes at me appreciatively, "You unbuttoned my jeans and had your hand down my pants in your sleep. That's not what I wanted from tonight, but you have no idea how it feels to hold you and have you want me."

I go to him and pull the blankets back to find his jeans unbuttoned and his hand wrapped around Tiger. I kiss Danny on the cheek, then gently on the lips. Again I go to his lips and press my own to his. I gaze into his eyes for something, anything. His smile and the happiness starts to shine in his eyes as I catch a glimpse of my own reflection there. "I've missed you, Danny. Let's make us both happy." I straddle him right where he is and claim his mouth with mine. He moves his hands to my hips and Tiger has joined the party. I move over him and Tiger is hard at my entrance. He's kissing me back now and I hope I haven't pushed him too far, but it's what he needs, what we need. I slide down allowing Tiger entrance and take him slowly, remembering how big he is.

"Oh, Jacks. Fuck, you're better than I remember. You're perfect." I push myself down farther, taking him all the way and he moans, calling out my name. "It's been me and my hand for three years. This isn't going to go well, you need to get off me." I move on him slowly, sliding up and down his amazing shaft and feeling him stretch me, grinding against him, losing my mind. "Jacks, I can't take a chance and get you pregnant."

"It's okay baby, I got on the pill. I want you to know how it feels to come inside. Nobody else will ever get to. Only you, Danny. Let me take care of you and show you how special you are. Don't worry, just feel and be selfish, everything for you."

"Can't do it, Jacks. It means too much. No time..." and he picks me up off of him. Breathing hard, I put my mouth on his tip and stroke him with both hands until he cries out and comes hard in my mouth. He reaches for me and holds me tight. After a few minutes he whispers in my ear, "I can't, Jacks. Not until you're mine and we don't have to be a secret. I want you to be mine. I want things and it can't be a game."

"I'm sorry. I didn't mean to push you. You always make me lose my mind. It's only you, Danny. There's not another man out there for me, only you make me lose my mind saying and doing stupid things."

"I love that I'm the only one who makes you crazy, baby. Please understand why I can't go there no matter how much I want to." Danny kisses my cheek softly, then my collarbone while he runs his thumb across my lips. Then he finally gives in and does his Danny thing, pressing his lips to mine and moving his tongue over my lips telling me to part them for him. He slides his tongue into my mouth and I'm happy all over. His hands are a decadent treat caressing the sides of my body, touching me softly and deliberately while he's remembering my every curve. I pushed him and I shouldn't have. I can't comprehend where his mind is and his life is more serious, it has to be. He has responsibilities I can't possibly understand because I've

never taken care of anyone, only myself. Of course he's going
to take sex more seriously than he did in the past. His kiss
becomes more aggressive and demanding. Danny holds my
naked body tight to his own and rolls me underneath him
without breaking our heated kiss. I missed this! His weight on
me is luxurious. He whispers in my ear, "You weren't ready for
me before. I need to fix that," he says. He delicately caresses
my sex and he slides in two fingers. "You're so hot and wet.
You need this as much as I do. I didn't realize you were waiting
for me. One of the reasons I quit calling was that I didn't want
to hold you back, I wanted you to live even if I couldn't." He
rubs my sensitive nub lightly and has me whimpering instantly.
"Not yet, baby." He slides in a third finger and strokes me. He
claims my mouth with his and his heart's pounding. He takes
his hand away and slides his hard cock into me, still kissing me
like he'll never stop and he needs me to breathe. He moves
slowly and deliberately, pushing in completely and pulling all
the way out, repeatedly. The heat and friction between us is
insane. My body is on edge and ready to explode, every touch
another step closer to detonation. Danny reaches between my
legs and rubs my clit while he continues with his tongue and
hard length. My cries of pleasure are captured by his mouth and
his smile of satisfaction is pressed against my lips. He sits up,
pulling his mouth away from me, moving faster and deeper.
Hitting my magic spot over and over, intensifying my orgasm. I
call out his name with every pass and it drives him to take me
harder, pounding into me with abandon. "Oh, fuck!" he pulls
out quickly, releasing on my inner thigh. His heavy body on top
of me, he lies there with his arms around me. "You make me
forget what I'm doing and forget my life. I need more of you.
No matter what happens, I still love you, Jacks. Always." His

words make me smile uncontrollably and my heart goes skipping through a grassy meadow with balloons, singing little ditties about love. I cringe internally at the sound of the disclaimer, blocking the negative thoughts from my head and my heart. I get it. He doesn't have control over everything, but I'm willing to be his secret. Whatever it takes to have time with Danny.

The quiet alone time is almost deafening. I want to say things, but I don't want to spook him. I can tell he's antsy, probably always at work or with Jackie. Sometimes quiet time can mess with your head. Start a conversation. Something that'll help you get into the same space. "Are they still deciding on the menu for the Supper Club?"

"They aren't to that point yet. They've been sampling food and looking for someone they can name to be the chef for the Supper Club. I guess I was auditioning at the same time you were."

"I didn't know they do that. How does it work?"

"Since the Supper Club is new and started out as a show, the creator is treating the food like it's a cast member and wants it to fit in with the concept. They released the details to the kitchen staff and any of us who wanted to be chef of the Supper Club were told to submit a recipe. The recipes the crew wanted to try were scheduled to be served during auditions—that's what I was doing when you were on stage singing."

"What did you make?"

"I made a higher class version of my piggy mac."

"You can make your piggy mac better?" I ask him, not believing it.

Danny laughs at me and it makes me happy to see him loosening up. "That's what I'm working on. Tonight's had a different cheese combination. The one I served for the crew had bacon mixed into it and a lightly toasted garlic crouton."

"I don't get it. Why are you working on it now, when they've already tasted it?"

"Oh, the top three of us have each been asked to put together a menu. I'm expecting they will pick something off the menu they want to try, possibly multiple things. I want it to be perfect. It would be my first time as chef." Danny keeps his speech even as if it isn't a big deal.

"You made the top three! Your food is delicious. Why didn't you tell me? I'm excited for you, I know you've worked hard for this. Tell me about your menu."

"You already tasted half of it," he looks at me and smiles. "I almost forgot dessert." He gets out of bed, retrieves the container from the mini fridge and the bag he wasn't giving up earlier. Then the world became a better place as I sit in bed with Danny naked and he feeds me a bite of the most scrumptious fudgy chocolate and peanut butter blondie layered brownie with vanilla whipped cream. I may have died and gone to heaven. "Damn Jacks! Did I make you orgasm with my food? I swear you just moaned in pleasure." Danny sets the dessert aside and reaches for me, needing to kiss me, and wanting me to make those sounds for him. He presses his lips to mine gently, slowly tasting me and indulging himself. Sucking lightly and biting on my lower lip.

I'm startled when the phone rings and reach to answer it, but Danny stops me, "I gave Tony the number in case he needed to find me. He doesn't know I'm with you."

I answer the phone, and it's Dot checking in on me. I tell her I can't talk and I promise to call her tomorrow. She's satisfied, only wanting to confirm I'm still alive. I hang up and go back to

Danny, only to find him eating the brownie and whipped cream with a shit-eating grin on his face. "Oh, hell no! You better share!" I crowd him to get another bite and he starts talking again while he feeds me bite after bite of deliciousness.

"Why are you here through Tuesday? You never stayed here that long."

"I'm focusing on singing, since it's the other thing that makes me happy. I've been traveling for auditions because I'm not having any luck in Hollywood and LA. Challenging with my day job and the expense of travel, so I'm being picky about when and getting multiple auditions on each trip. This weekend Saturday through Tuesday in Vegas, I have six potential auditions. You were there for my first one and I got called back, they told me they'll be contacting me within a week to make me an offer. I'm still going to the others. Who knows what they'll offer me and maybe one of the others will be a better opportunity. A couple of the auditions are real close in time. I might not make both, but I'm going to give it a shot."

"Are you moving here?"

"I will if I get a long enough contract and it actually pays the bills. I can't imagine being able to support myself doing something I love. I enjoy my job at the warehouse and the ability to work with all the music, but to be able to sing would be amazing. I'm not expecting it to happen with my first job offer." I'm beyond excited by the idea. "Don't worry, Danny. I don't expect anything from you. I don't want to be a problem for you. This is simply a coincidence."

"Baby, don't worry about me. It makes me happy that you'll be closer. It means I'll see you, even when I can't be with you. Someday maybe we can be us."

"I don't know anything yet."

"I do, Jacks. I heard you up on the stage singing. Your first song was perfect for the Supper Club and your voice was crazy good. I didn't know how great you sing, I should've. And, I love how you gave them what they asked for. You didn't hesitate and try to sing something else that would be good for the Supper Club. Nobody else sang anything anywhere near Aerosmith. I loved it. It won't be long until you get what you want."

He believes in me. I'm happy and my emotions start to come back to me in a way they haven't in years. My heart's beating stronger. "It means a lot to me, you believing in me. You make me happy."

"What have you been doing to prepare and practice?" Danny asks.

"I've been singing with a few different bands playing in Hollywood, female back-up. I get to sing lead on a couple songs a night. For the most part, the bands aren't serious enough or just want a girl on the stage. I sing a lot with Bryan, he's been writing songs as if it's as easy as drinking a glass of water." I probably should've left most of that out.

"Bryan? Isn't that the guy who was at your door at 2am right after I met you? He's still around?"

"Yea, he's a friend." Don't ask. Don't ask. Don't ask.

Danny focuses on me, "Jacks, I didn't expect you to wait for me. Do you have a guy?"

I stare Danny square in the eyes because I refuse to lie to him, "No boyfriend. Guys from the bands tried to get me and I blew them off. Bryan wants me to be his, he tries hard and sometimes he can be persistent. When it had been a year since I'd heard from you and I didn't know how to reach you, I gave in to him hoping he might help me forget you. But, it didn't. It made me miss you more. I haven't been a perfect angel. I've had some drunk nights and most of them have been spent with

Bryan. It's been months since anything has happened. Now I know where you are and you aren't married. It'll only be you and I don't care if I'm a secret." My own words make my heart warm and I'm scared with Danny for the first time, without a lie between us.

"I don't want you to suffer because of me, Jacks. You don't have to live my life."

"I want to live your life, it's the only way I get to be with you. I believe in… someday."

I catch glimpses of my happy-go-lucky Danny, but mostly he's living the only way he knows how and getting through each day taking care of his daughter in the best way he's capable. There's no doubt Jackie's his everything, but her mother is a bitch and Danny doesn't deserve to be controlled even if he did knock her up. It takes two people. I wouldn't be surprised if she did it on purpose to trap him. Danny's a stand-up guy and you can depend on him. I bet she was surprised when he didn't marry her, but it's his general character to do the right thing and not lead her on. He couldn't keep up his end of the marriage, he'd be lying to her, and he couldn't make vows he didn't believe in his heart. Jackie is lucky to have him, he'll always be there for her. There needs to be a way I can be there for him and he can get away. I guess this is the best we can do, for now.

I lean in to kiss him on the lips and snuggle my head into his shoulder. He wraps his arms around me and pulls me close to his body while he slides us down to the pillow and hides us under the blankets. I fall asleep there, wrapped in his body and his loving arms, laying on his chest listening to his heartbeat.

I allow myself to dream about how life would be if Danny and I both get the Supper Club gigs. The idea alone makes me giddy. Can you imagine Danny being the chef, creating the menu with his recipes and his food getting served to everyone, while I'm on stage singing? Being at the same place together and doing what makes us happy. The possibility of stealing away time to be alone together secretly with his arms around me, naked, and searching for the path to our someday. It would be amazing even if he had to go home to her and not with me. At least we'd get time for our happy.

CHAPTER TWENTY-SIX

I wake up early because I have to pee and set an alarm to make sure I get up in time to be ready for auditions. I tap Danny on the arm to ask if he needs an alarm set, and I'm surprised when he speaks without opening his eyes, "Good morning, my angel. Do you want to get in bed with Daddy or watch cartoons?" He isn't talking to me and I'm not sure if I should respond. "Jackie? Where are you?" he asks with urgency and still not opening his eyes. I climb back into bed next to him, his warm body against mine. Danny opens his eyes and sits up straight, startled, checking out his surroundings. "Where am I?"

I sit up next to him and run my hand down his cheek, "Hey, Danny. I'm right here." He turns to me, "You stayed the night with me at Excalibur."

"Jacks? It's really you?" He caresses my face gently with his fingers.

"Yes, Danny. It's really us." I can't control the smile on my face. I understand exactly what he's going through. You start to wonder if you're in the real world or your dream world where things come true that'll probably never happen. We both felt the same way—we were never going to be together again, not even in the same room—yet here we are. Danny responds without words. There's no other way to say it, he attacks me. His sexy tiger tattoo suddenly grows horns and I'm the prey. He's hot, horny, hard, and demanding in this sleepy state he's in. He pulls me over to his lap and kisses me with crazy heat, licking, nibbling, biting, driving me out of my mind. His heated hands roam my body, exploring every part of me, squeezing my ass, teasing my breasts, pinching my nipples. His hard, growing cock causes him to move uncomfortably, adjusting how he has me sitting on his lap and having trouble. Finally, there he is, my sexy Danny with need in his eyes and my belly flutters in anticipation.

"Fuck it!" and he starts to slide into me. "Jacks, you're fucking amazing. I never should've let you go. Only me and you from now on, baby. No one else will have me and I don't want anyone else to have you. I want you, baby. I don't want to be miserable anymore." He keeps pushing up into me and goes back to kissing me, hard and demanding, wet, sucking on my tongue, claiming my mouth over and over while I'm mounted on his cock and he has all the control. He moves his hands to my hips and pushes me down on him, he's desperate to get in further and can't get there no matter what he does. He moves me to get me straddling him in the best position and spreads my legs as far as he can on his mission to get in deep. Taking my hips and pushing me down again, he moves his hand down to my sex, finding how tight I am around his huge cock and it makes him harder. He finds my center, pressing and rubbing, setting me off with no effort at all. My body convulses around his cock and he's almost too big as my body rolls in an uncontrollable pleasure. He keeps kissing me, pushing up into me and moaning. "You're amazing. Nothing better than you getting off on me." He reaches for my sex again and starts to rub my sensitive nub.

I cry out, "No, too much."

Danny holds me tight to his body, "You're fine, Jacks. Everything is fine. I have you. We're together. Give yourself to me, baby. I'll take care of you." I let go at his will. He sets me off again and again and again. I'm screaming out his name and raking his back mindlessly. He quickly rolls me under him and slams into me repeatedly, exploring me and setting me off again in the process. I swear he has magic hands. "Oh Jacks. I need this baby. I need you."

"Anything for you, Danny. Whatever you want, it's okay. I want you to have it." The words come out of my mouth and I mean them.

Danny slides in and out, he's ready to go and he reaches for his cock numerous times, but never takes it in his hand. "Damn it, you make me crazy, Jacks." He slams in hard and he's better than anything I've experienced before, when he releases the most manly guttural groan and pulses inside me. I touch myself because I'm on the edge and want to be with him in the moment. I set myself off with Danny still inside me and he cries out, "Oh, fuck me!" he strokes in and pulls out a few more times before he pushes all the way in and holds me to him, not letting me go.

———

When my alarm goes off, I wake up to find Danny wrapped around me and still inside me—apparently happy to be there.

Danny gazes at me and grins, showing me traces of my happy-go-lucky Danny, "Jacks, I meant everything I said to you. It's going to take me some time, but please don't give up on me. You inspire me to live. Living means I'm with you."

MUFFIN MAN

A Novella

Robbi

"Everybody out!" The manager yells, running through the salon as we all ignore her. She's not the owner. Problem is the owner is out of town and she's in charge. She stops and at the top of her lungs, "Evacuate now! It's going to explode!"

The salon freezes instantly, the calm before the storm. There's a sudden frenzy of women gathering their necessities, and their clients as they run outside hysterically. I casually get up out of the salon chair and walk out with Deanna, my stylist, close behind me, and avoid the trampling stampede of frantic, high-pitched women.

We all gather outside for the details, but the manager is still in there! She comes running out with the massage therapists and their clients wrapped in robes. It triggers me to survey the scene for what stages of beautification we're all in. I mean, we all go to the salon for different things. Personally, it's how I stay blonde and that's not changing any time soon because I can prove blondes have more fun. The stylists are brushing out their hair, fixing their make-up, taking off aprons. I overhear what's happening and empathize for some of the poor women in the middle of getting services, when it hits me—I'm one of them.

The building had started to make a banging noise. The manager, Shawna, had taken it upon herself to find the problem. She was left in charge after all and the ship was not going to sink under her direction. This isn't some basic barbershop, this is Michelle's Salon and Shawna would not be responsible for damage to the custom European style decor Michelle has taken years to refine. It was the water heater. The water heater was making the loud noise, like it had air in the line or was trying to pass bad Chinese food. It was also emitting gas fumes and sparked every time there was a bang. The bangs were getting more frequent.

Which brings us to the bunch of women now standing outside in the shade of the building's front awning. It's almost lunchtime and the parking lot of the strip mall is starting to fill up with patrons to the food establishments, eyes peering at the motley crowd of women in smocks milling around helplessly. Shawna's on the phone with 911 trying to get, yes, you guessed it, the fire department.

911: What's your emergency?
Shawna: There's going to be a fire
911: Is there a fire now?
Shawna: No, not yet.
911: Sorry, we can't help you yet
click

At least, that's how I imagine it from the story Shawna told. There were others calling, it would be fine. Help would show up. Hopefully. Deanna, the only person I will let near my hair, is getting fidgety and twirling her soft brunette curls between her fingers. "I'm sure they'll be here quick. We still have ten minutes before we have to wash the bleach out of your hair. Everything will be fine." For those of you who are not salon savvy, leaving chemicals on your hair too long isn't good. Hair will break off, fall out, burn. I've seen it smoke. All kinds of horrible things, and I take pride in my long platinum blonde hair. So, let me translate what Deanna said: Ten minutes until utter disaster. Others have half a haircut, shampoo or conditioner in their hair, extensions partially tied in. The people who were getting massages are relaxed, even if their clothes are inside the building and they're outside wearing only a robe.

Everyone that could primp, had primped for the firemen to show up. It's a lineup and I can imagine the firemen walking the line, *"I'll take this one, and this one. You don't mind sharing, right?"* The senior firefighter steps up and says, *"Sorry, I get first choice. Seniority gets perks. I'll be taking this one from you."* Anyway, you get the idea. It's a beauty pageant and then there's me with a plastic bag on my head and a lady with foils sticking up off her head like she could receive radio transmission.

The sound of sirens fill the air as the long red ladder truck pulls into the parking lot, stopping in front of the salon. The important thing here is the possible fire, but I appreciate firemen as much as the next girl, maybe more. Definitely more. I love a hot guy, even on days like today when I only get to drool from a distance because I look like a bag lady compared to the stylists. The first guy is a bit older with short salt and pepper hair. He's fit and fills his navy blue uniform nicely. The second guy is shorter, still at least 5'9" and wearing one of those bulky yellow jackets with reflectors. His face is adorable, but the jacket hides everything else—not a hint of a single ab or muscular arm. The third reminds me of Goldilocks, he's just right. Thick, dirty blonde hair and the mustache to match. His navy blue uniform pants are topped with his station T-shirt which stretches across his chest and shoulders, yet loose where it's tucked into his Dickies. I'm busy imagining the things I could do to him. Naked. With my tongue. Deanna stomps her boots and drags me into the dog groomer next door.

"Firemen? Hot firemen?" I whined questioningly, not wanting to give up my view.

THE SWEET SPOT

An All About the Diamond Romance, #1

Can her baseball fantasy become reality, or will she strike out at love?

Rick Seno is a sexy warrior behind the plate in his catcher's gear. In control and calling the game for the San Diego Seals. He'd show me the same attention in my bed, if he was more than my imaginary baseball boyfriend.

I've worn a Seno jersey to every game since Rick became a big leaguer. It's silly. I'm almost a decade older than him. I don't compare to the flawless baseball skanks who wait for him at the player's garage.

But, what am I supposed to do when the All-Star of my dreams invites me out after a game?

I can't believe he wants me. Until tonight, I was completely content with my life. Now, I'm caught off base and I'm not sure I can make it home safe.

ACKNOWLEDGMENTS

This is the second book I wrote and I've kept it to myself, holding it close to my heart. Now it's book five in release order. Thank you to my dear author friends for giving me the confidence to move forward. I cherish your words of wisdom, camaraderie, comic relief, and dirty minds.

Thank you to my sister for not killing me when I held on to Danny for myself.

Thank you to my Naughties for brightening every single day with hotness and wit, especially Queen Admin Sam and Cheer Captain Alisa. You are all the best! Marybells, Carolyn, Jann, Jaime, Lynn, beta readers, supporters, bloggers, and of course my fab readers.

Never give up on your dreams. Do what makes you happy.

ABOUT THE AUTHOR

Naomi Springthorp is an emerging author. Just a California Girl is her fifth release. She's also writing other contemporary romance novels and novellas featuring baseball, firemen, and more.

Naomi is a born and raised Southern California girl. She lives with her husband and her feline fur babies. She believes that life has a soundtrack and half of the year should be spent cheering for her favorite baseball team.

Join her newsletter at
www.naomispringthorp.com/sign-up

ALSO BY NAOMI SPRINGTHORP

AN ALL ABOUT THE DIAMOND ROMANCE

The Sweet Spot

King of Diamonds

Diamonds in Paradise (a novella)

Star Crossed in the Outfield… coming 2/2019

The Closer (a novella)… coming 4/2019

Up at Bat… coming 2019

Stalking Second… coming 2019

NOVELLAS AND STANDALONE NOVELS

Muffin Man (a novella)

BETTING ON LOVE (VEGAS ROMANCE)

Just a California Girl

Jacks!… coming in 2019

OTHER NOVELLAS AND STANDALONE NOVELS

Confessions of an Online Junkie… coming soon

Finally in Focus (a novella)… coming soon

Made in the USA
San Bernardino, CA
14 January 2019